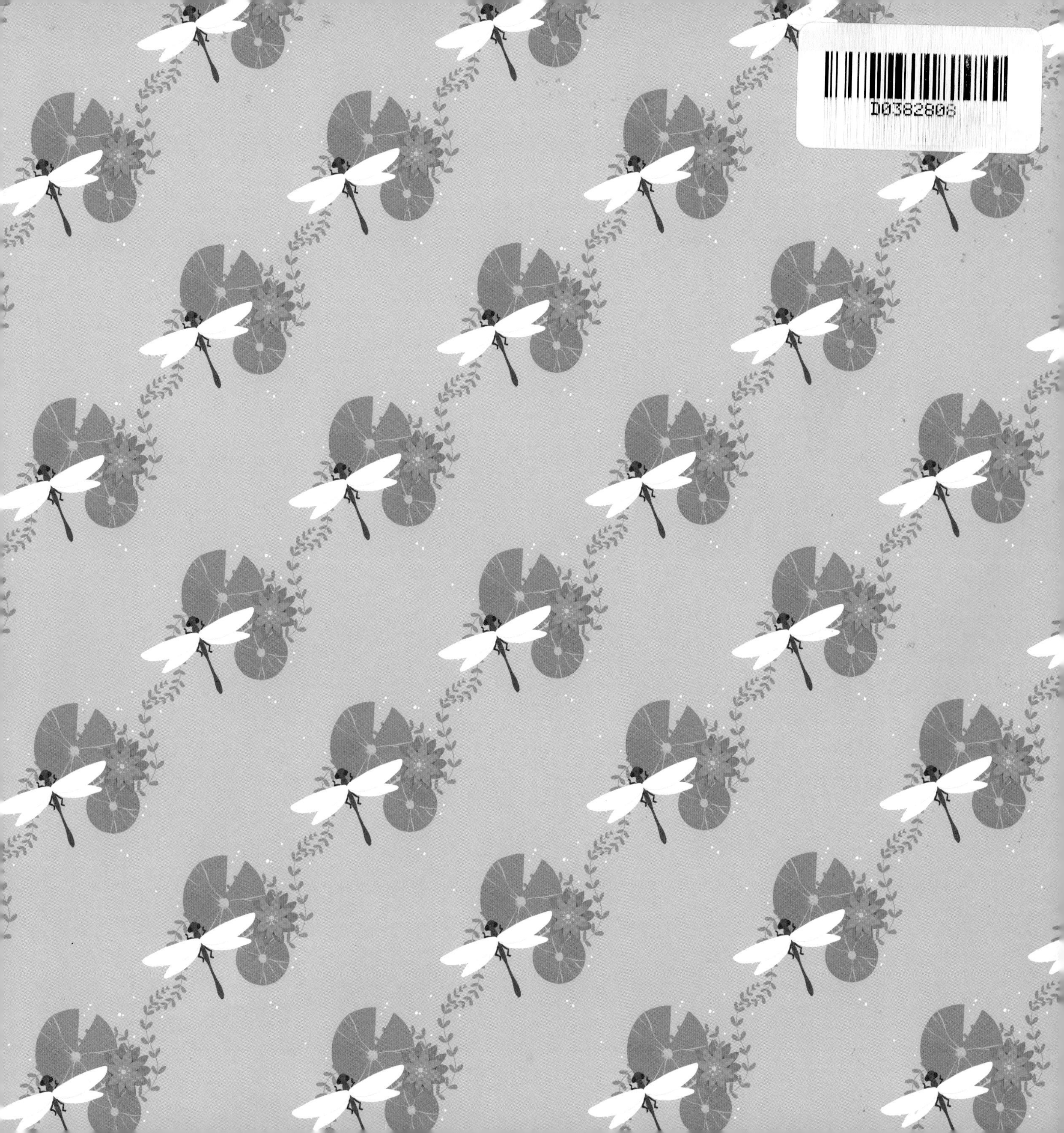

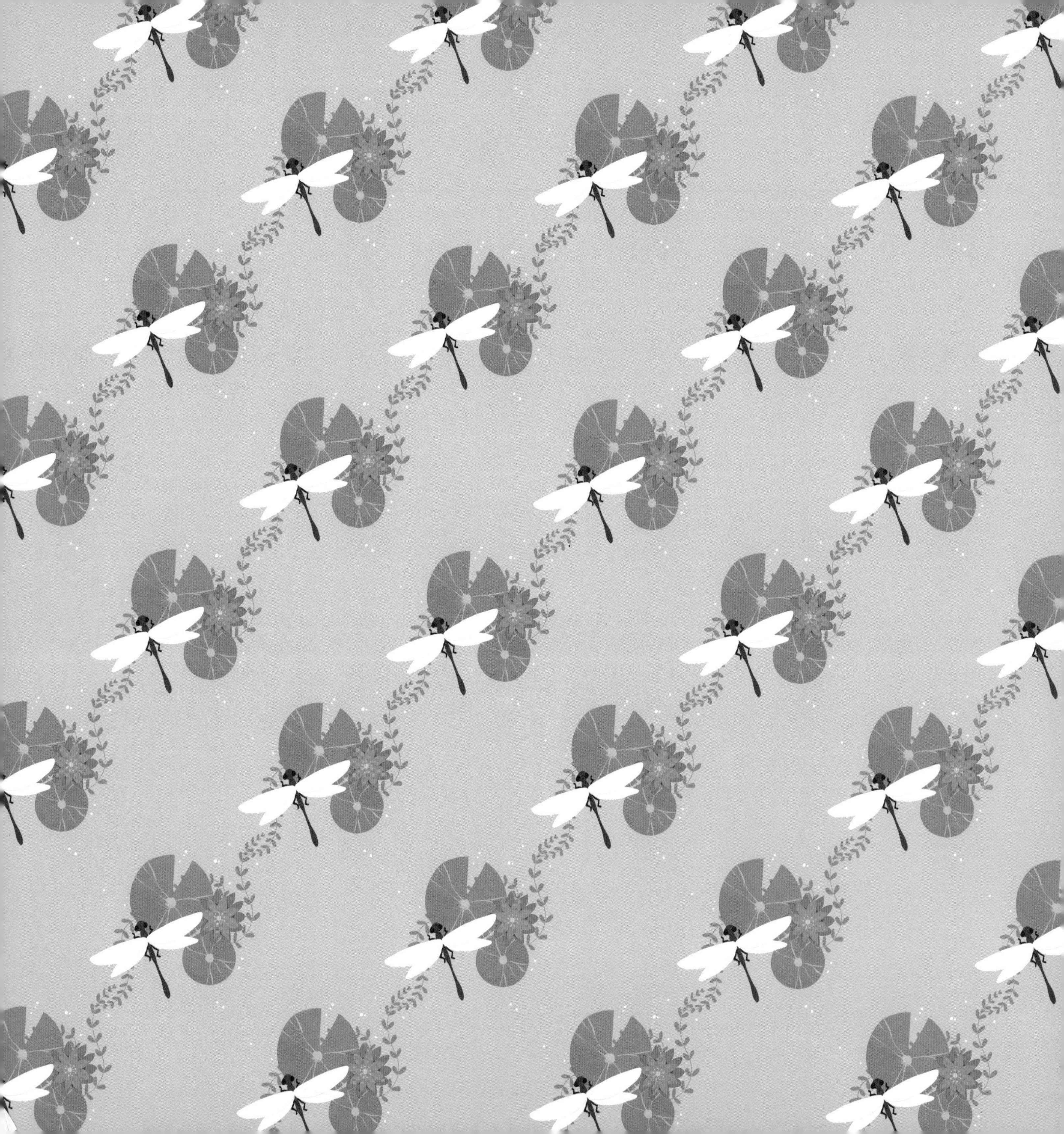

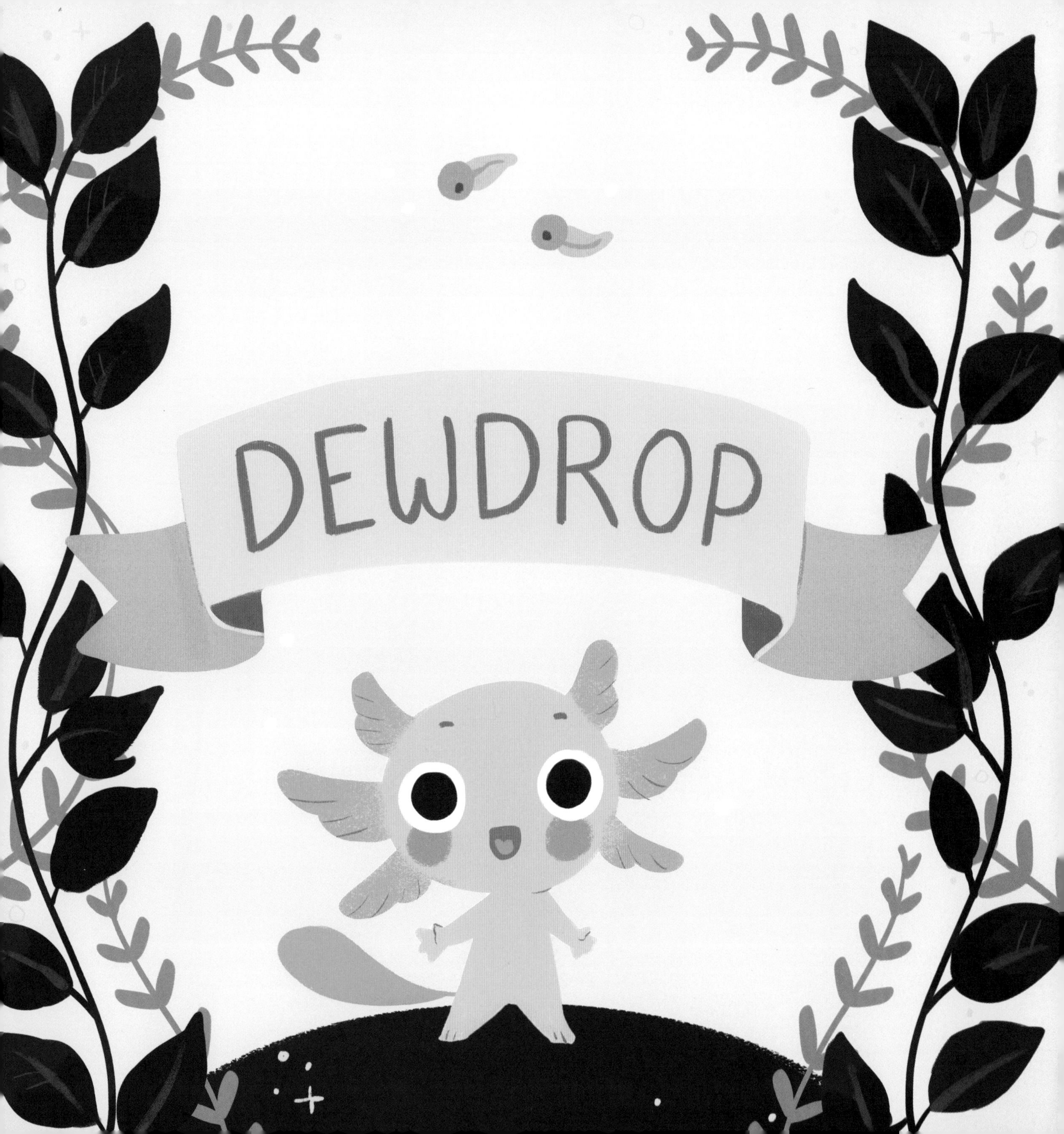
DEWDROP

DEWDROP

BY
Katie O'Neill

EDITED BY
Ari Yarwood

DESIGNED BY
Sonja Synak

ONI PRESS

AN ONI PRESS PUBLICATION

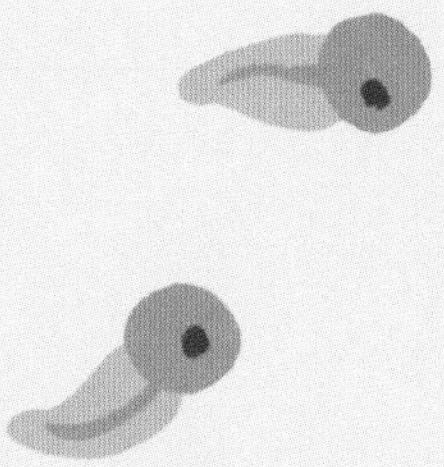

Published by Oni Press, Inc.

Published by Oni-Lion Forge Publishing Group, LLC
James Lucas Jones, *president & publisher*
Sarah Gaydos, *editor in chief*
Charlie Chu, *e.v.p. of creative & business development*
Brad Rooks, *director of operations*
Amber O'Neill, *special projects manager*
Harris Fish, *events manager*
Margot Wood, *director of marketing & sales*
Jeremy Atkins, *director of brand communications*
Devin Funches, *sales & marketing manager*
Katie Sainz, *marketing manager*
Tara Lehmann, *marketing & publicity associate*
Troy Look, *director of design & production*
Kate Z. Stone, *senior graphic designer*
Sonja Synak, *graphic designer*
Hilary Thompson, *graphic designer*
Angie Knowles, *digital prepress lead*
Shawna Gore, *senior editor*
Robin Herrera, *senior editor*
Amanda Meadows, *senior editor*
Jasmine Amiri, *editor*
Grace Bornhoft, *editor*
Zack Soto, *editor*
Steve Ellis, *vice president of games*
Ben Eisner, *game developer*
Michelle Nguyen, *executive assistant*
Jung Lee, *logistics coordinator*

Joe Nozemack, *publisher emeritus*

onipress.com | lionforge.com
facebook.com/onipress | facebook.com/lionforge
twitter.com/onipress | twitter.com/lionforge
instagram.com/onipress | instagram.com/lionforge

ktoneill.com
twitter.com/strangelykatie

First Edition: April 2020
ISBN: 978-1-62010-689-1
eISBN: 978-1-62010-701-0

Library of Congress Control Number: 2019939961

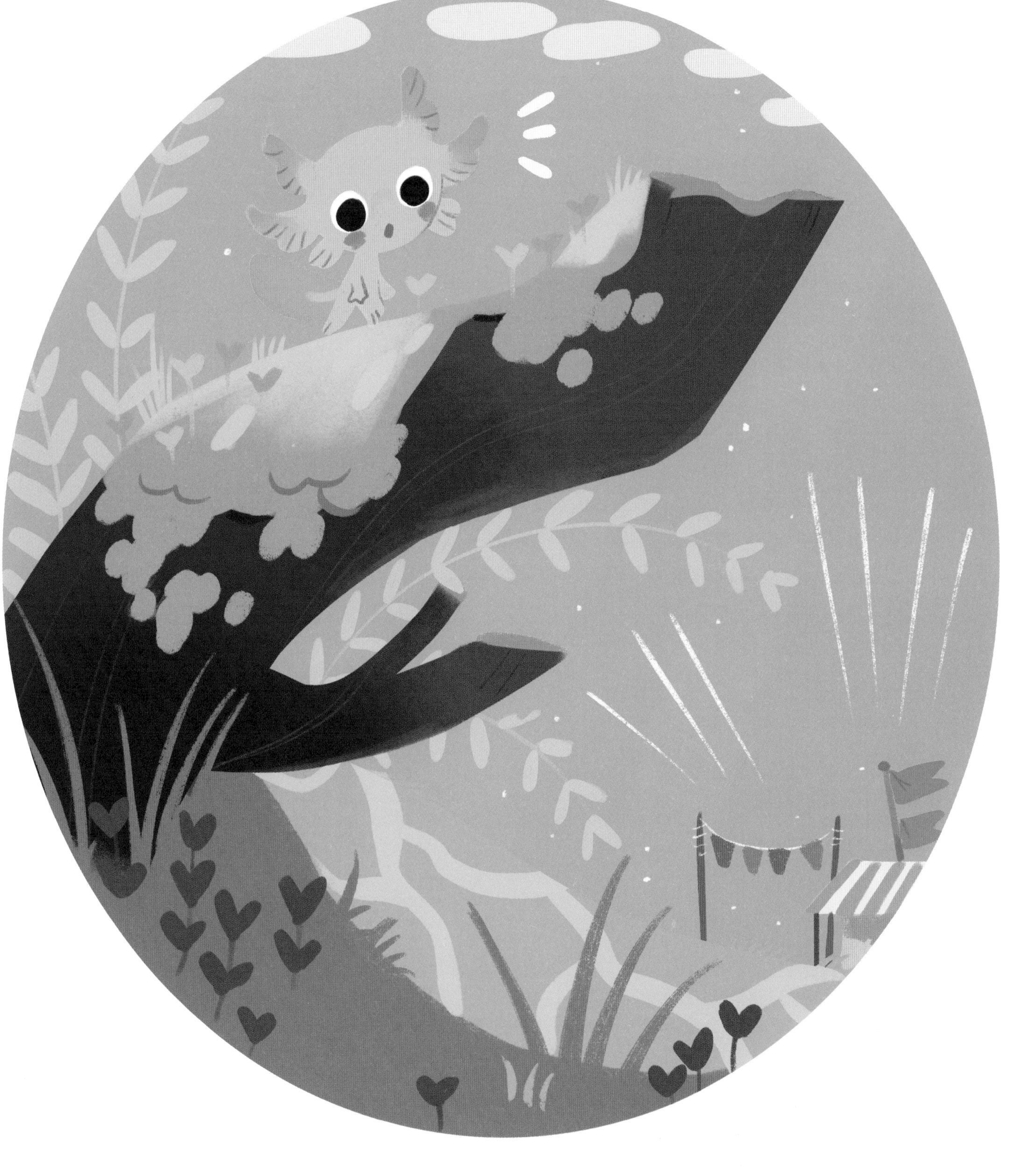

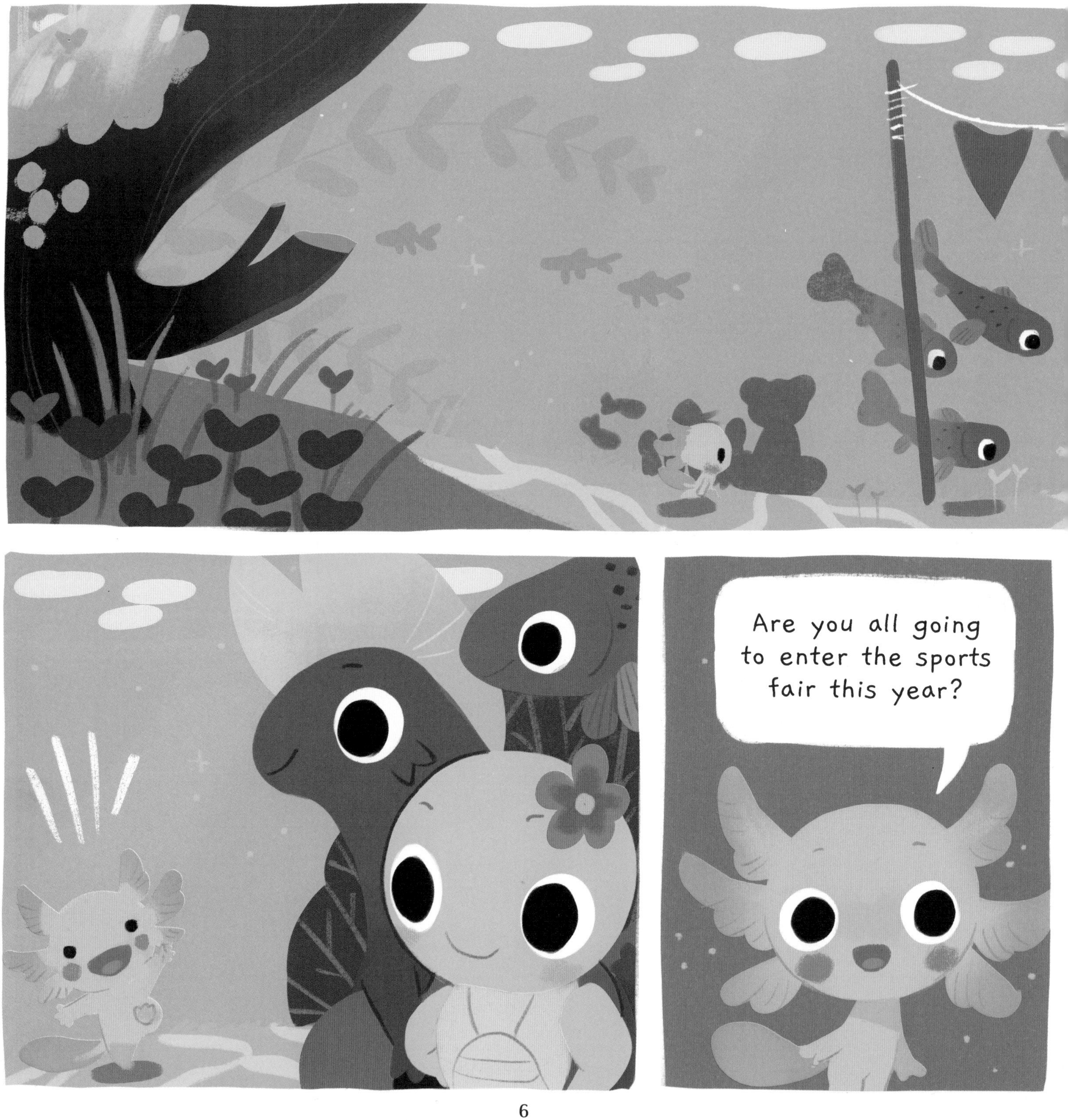
Are you all going to enter the sports fair this year?

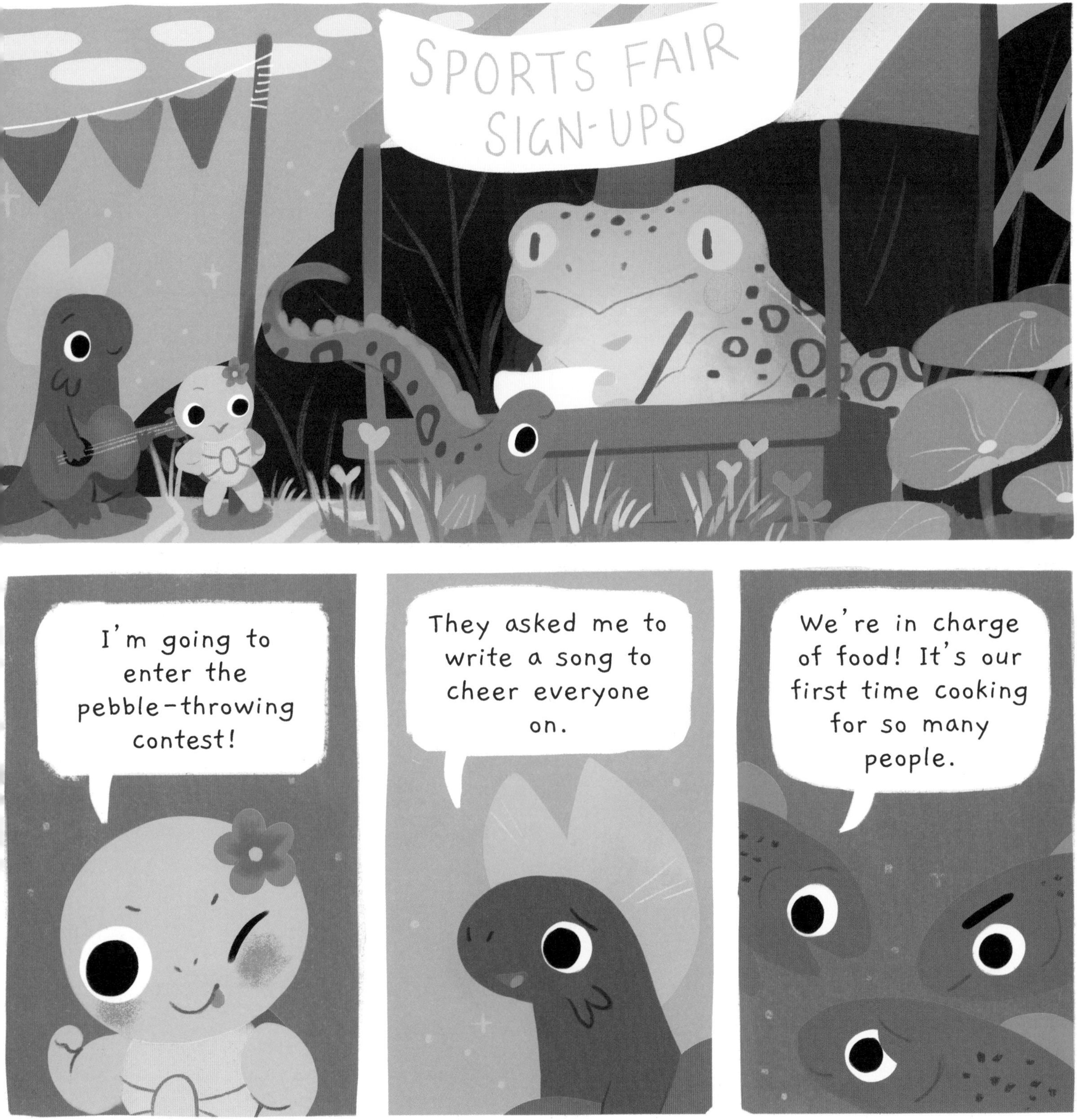
SPORTS FAIR SIGN-UPS
I'm going to enter the pebble-throwing contest!
They asked me to write a song to cheer everyone on.
We're in charge of food! It's our first time cooking for so many people.

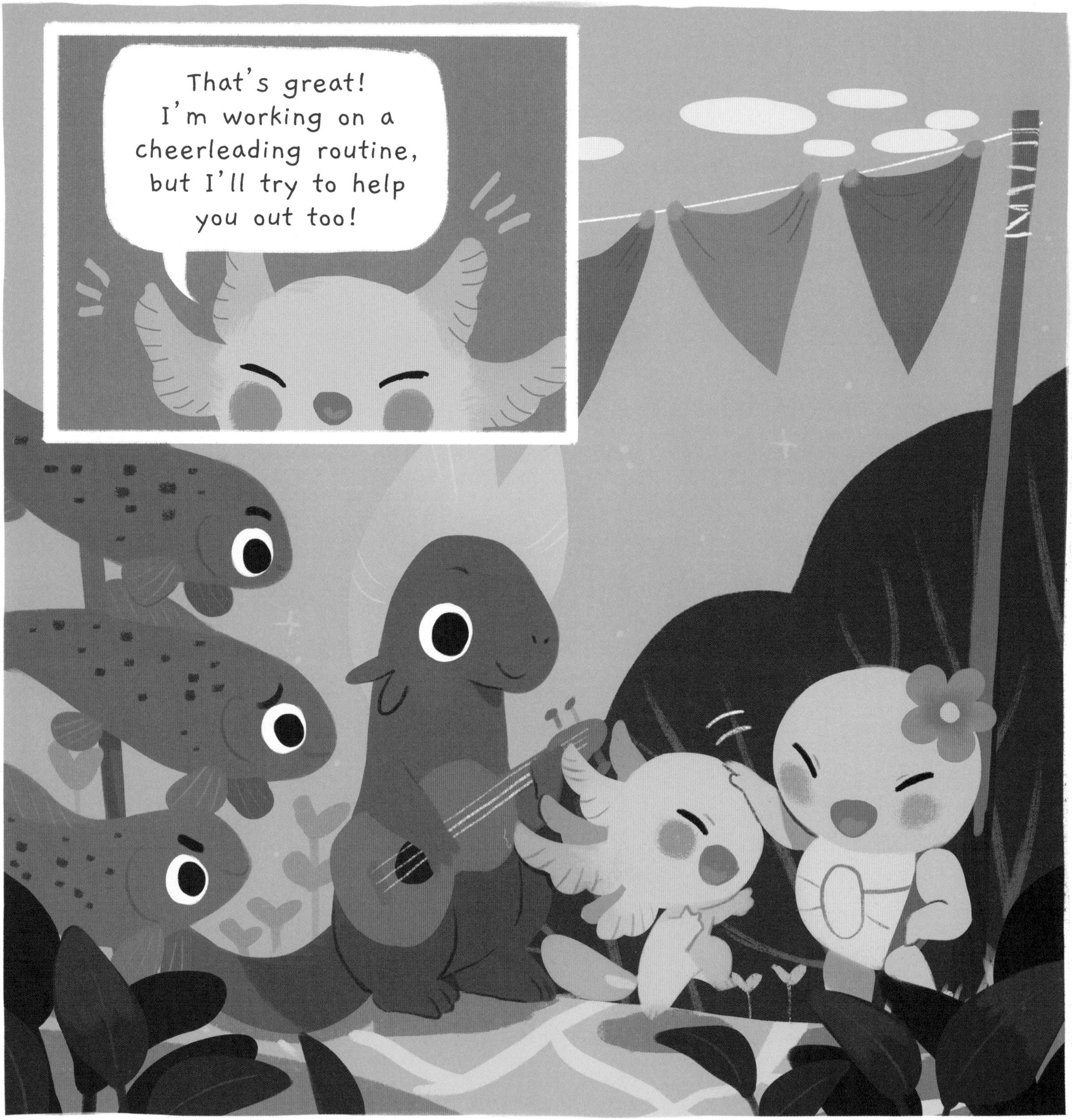
That's great! I'm working on a cheerleading routine, but I'll try to help you out too!

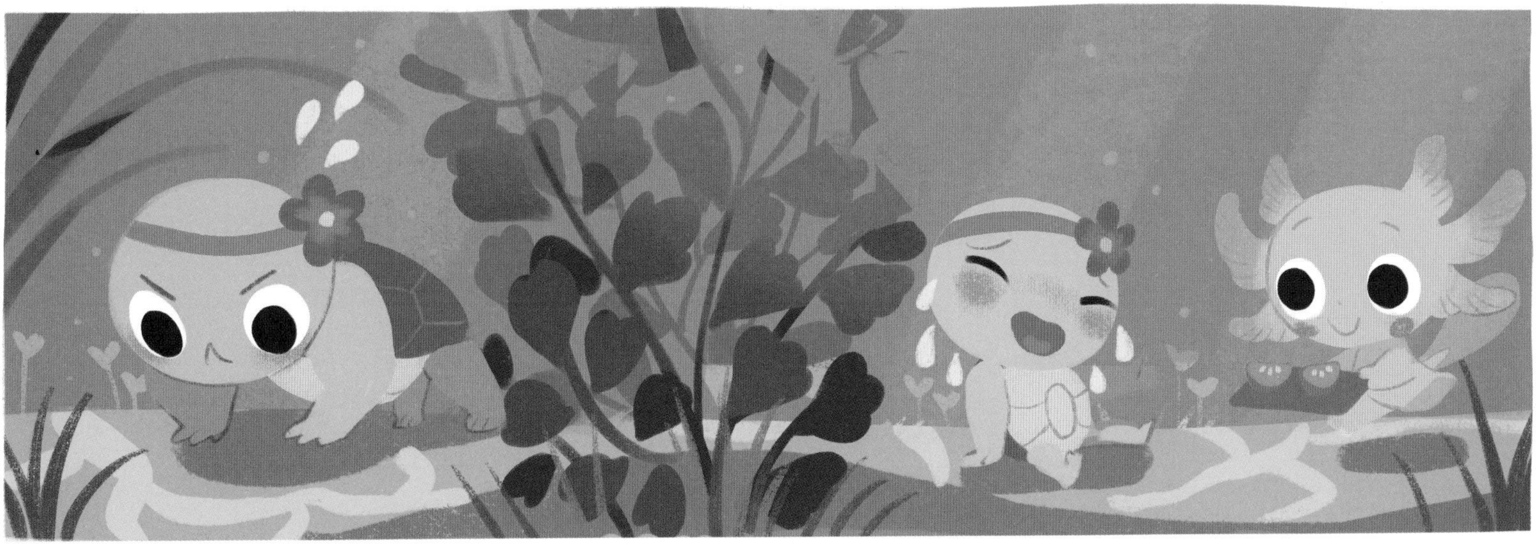

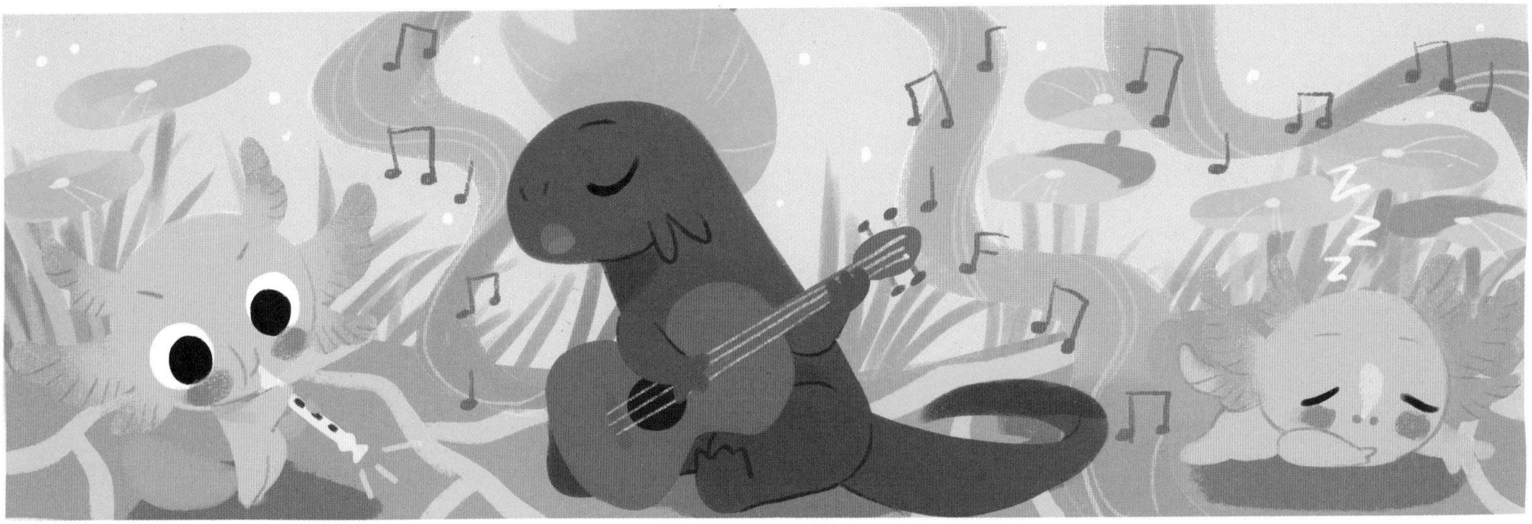

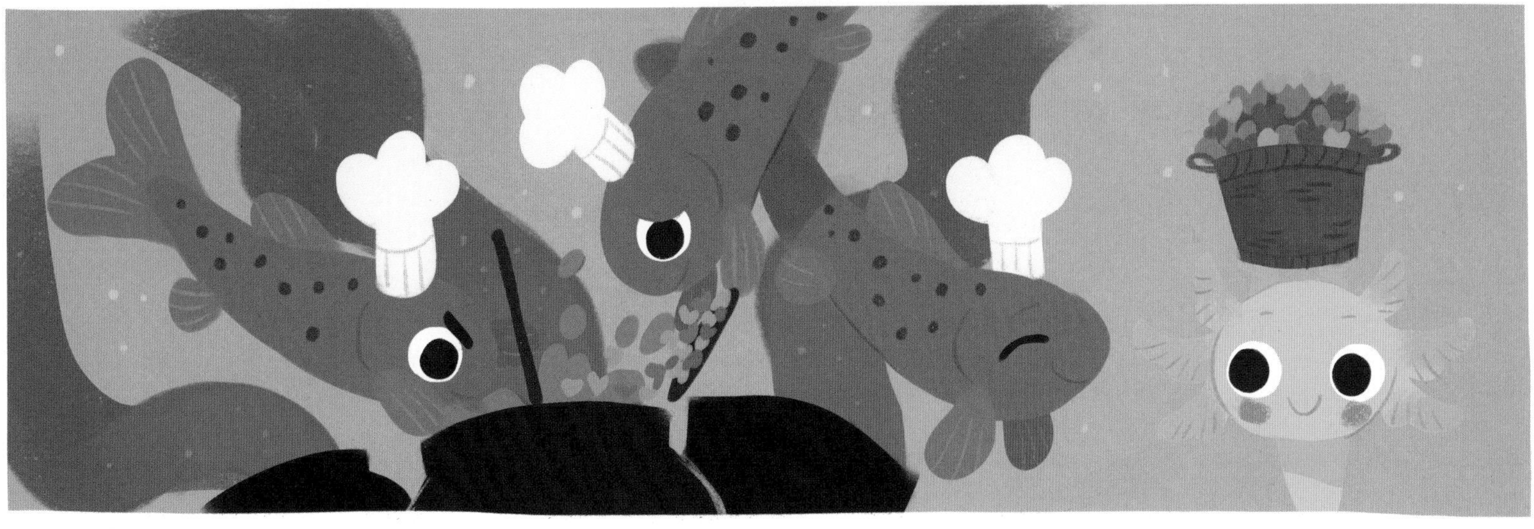

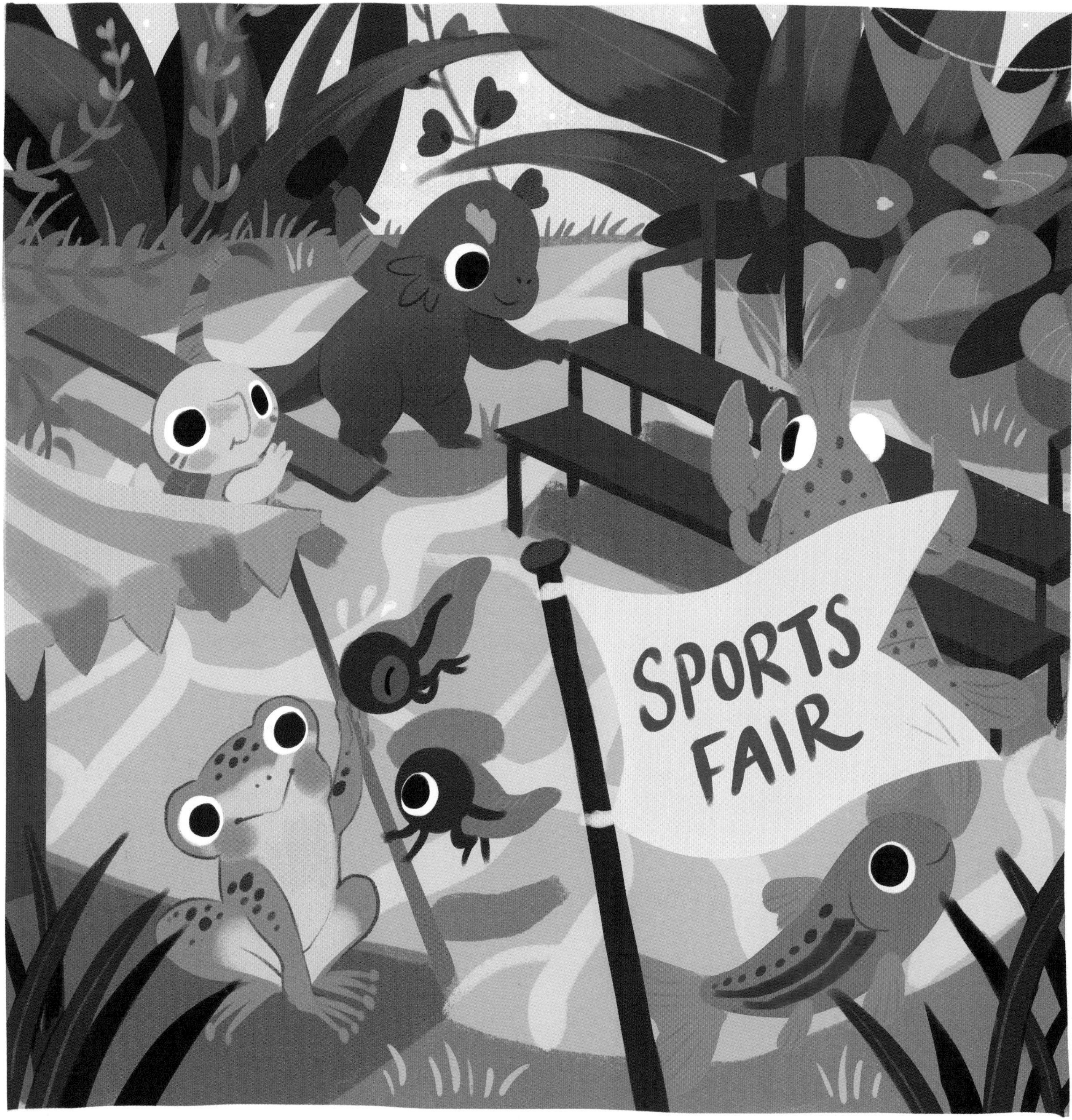
SPORTS
FAIR

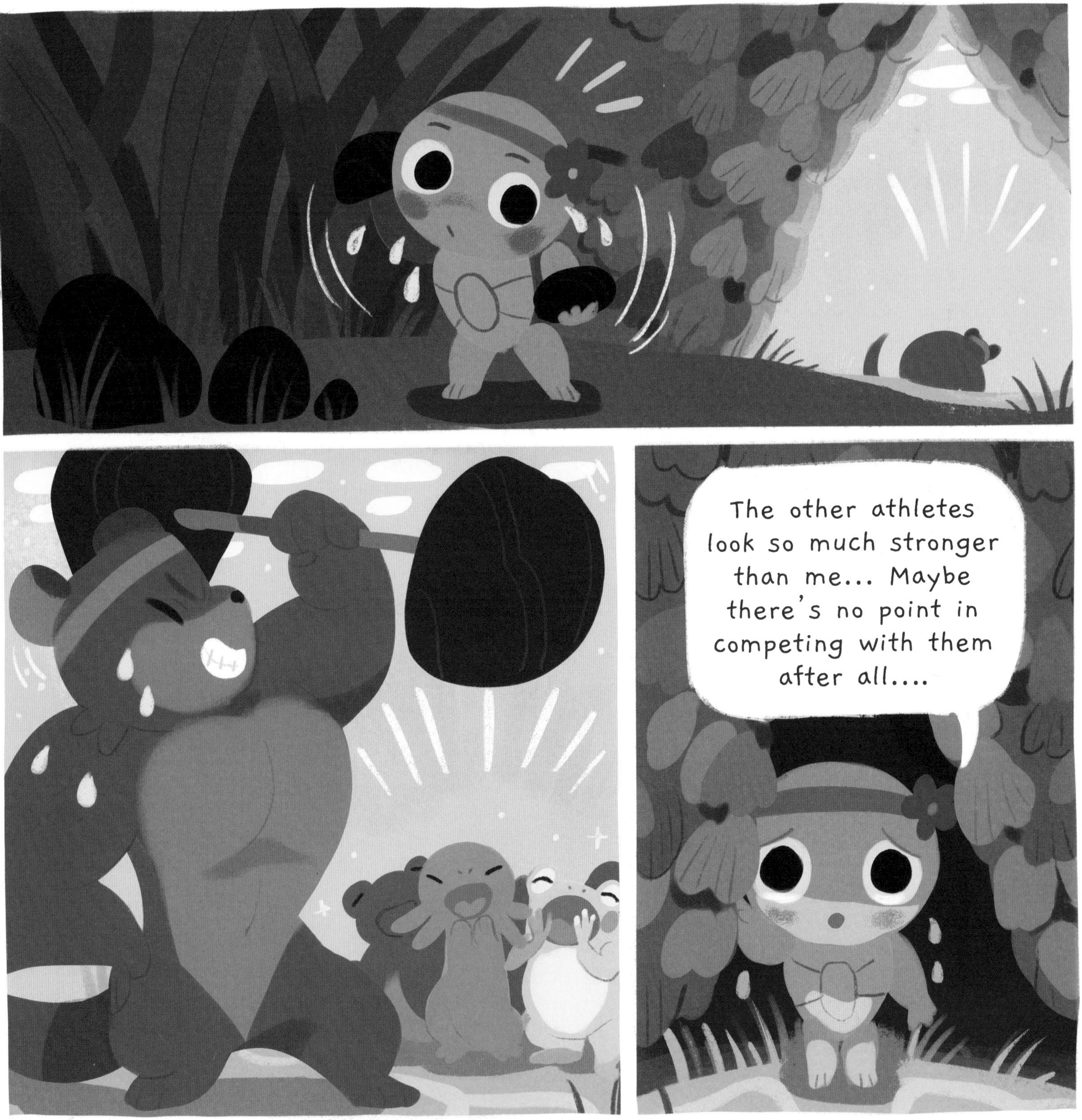
The other athletes look so much stronger than me... Maybe there's no point in competing with them after all....

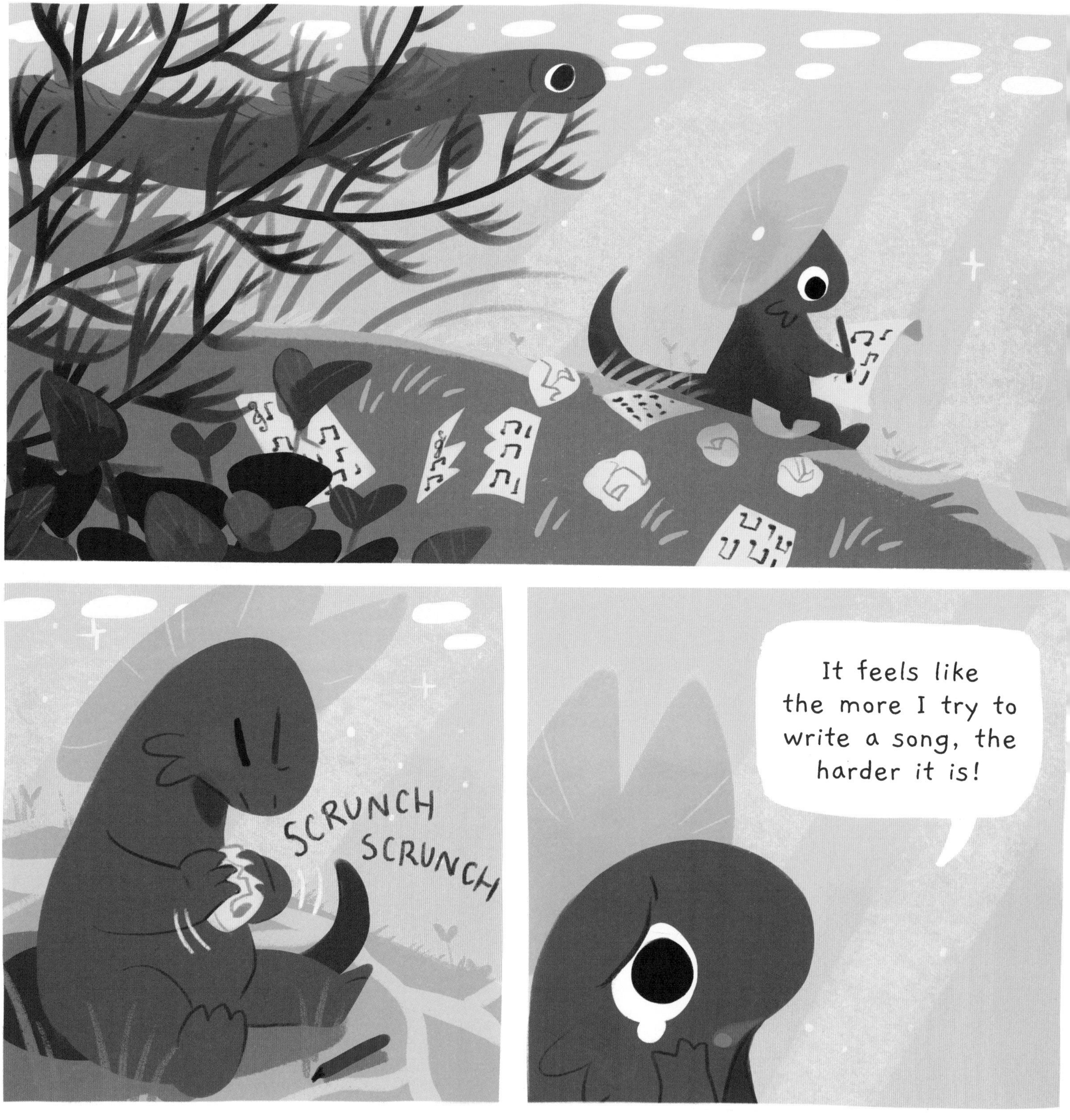
SCRUNCH
SCRUNCH
It feels like the more I try to write a song, the harder it is!

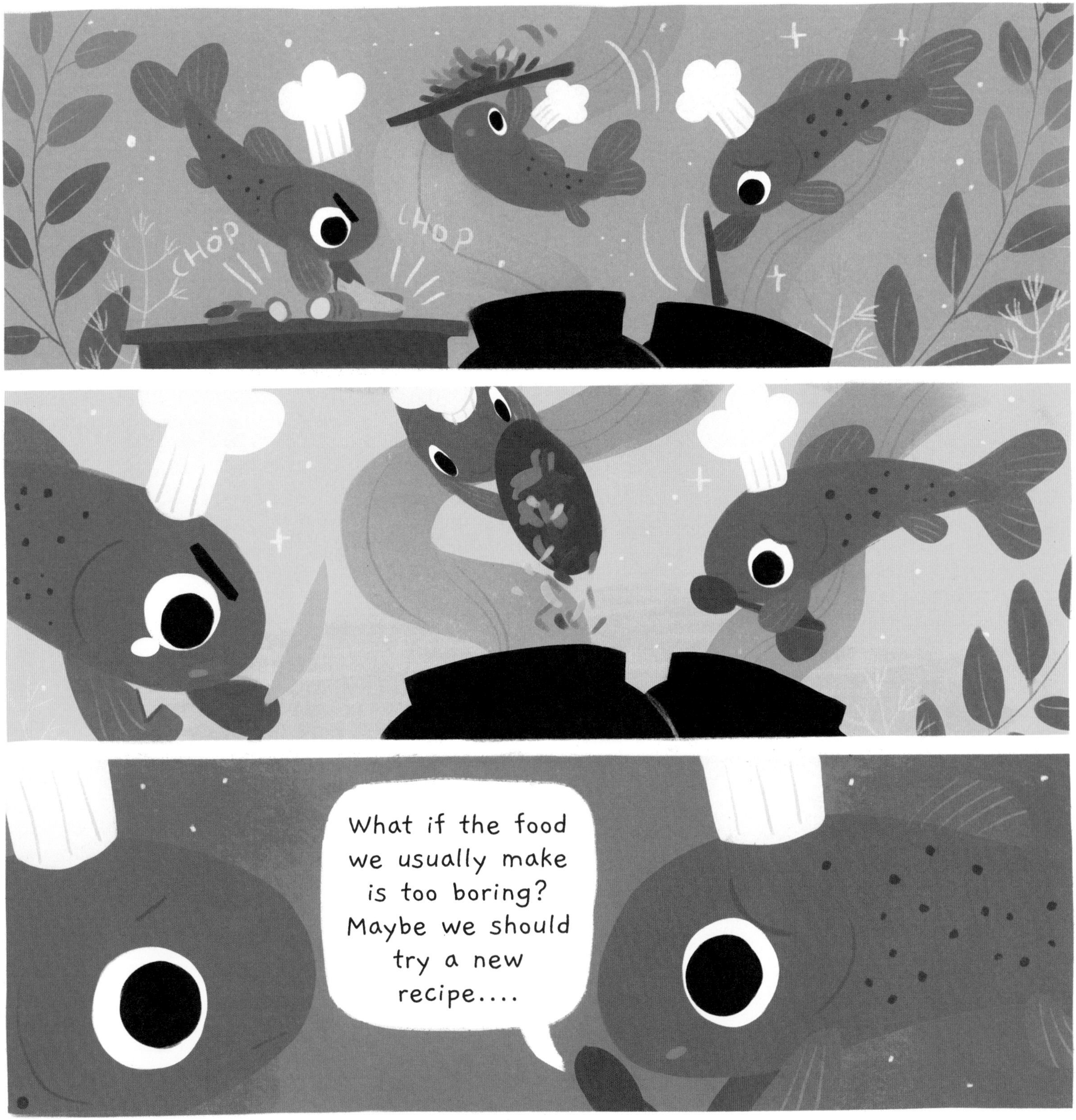
CHOP
CHOP
What if the food we usually make is too boring? Maybe we should try a new recipe....

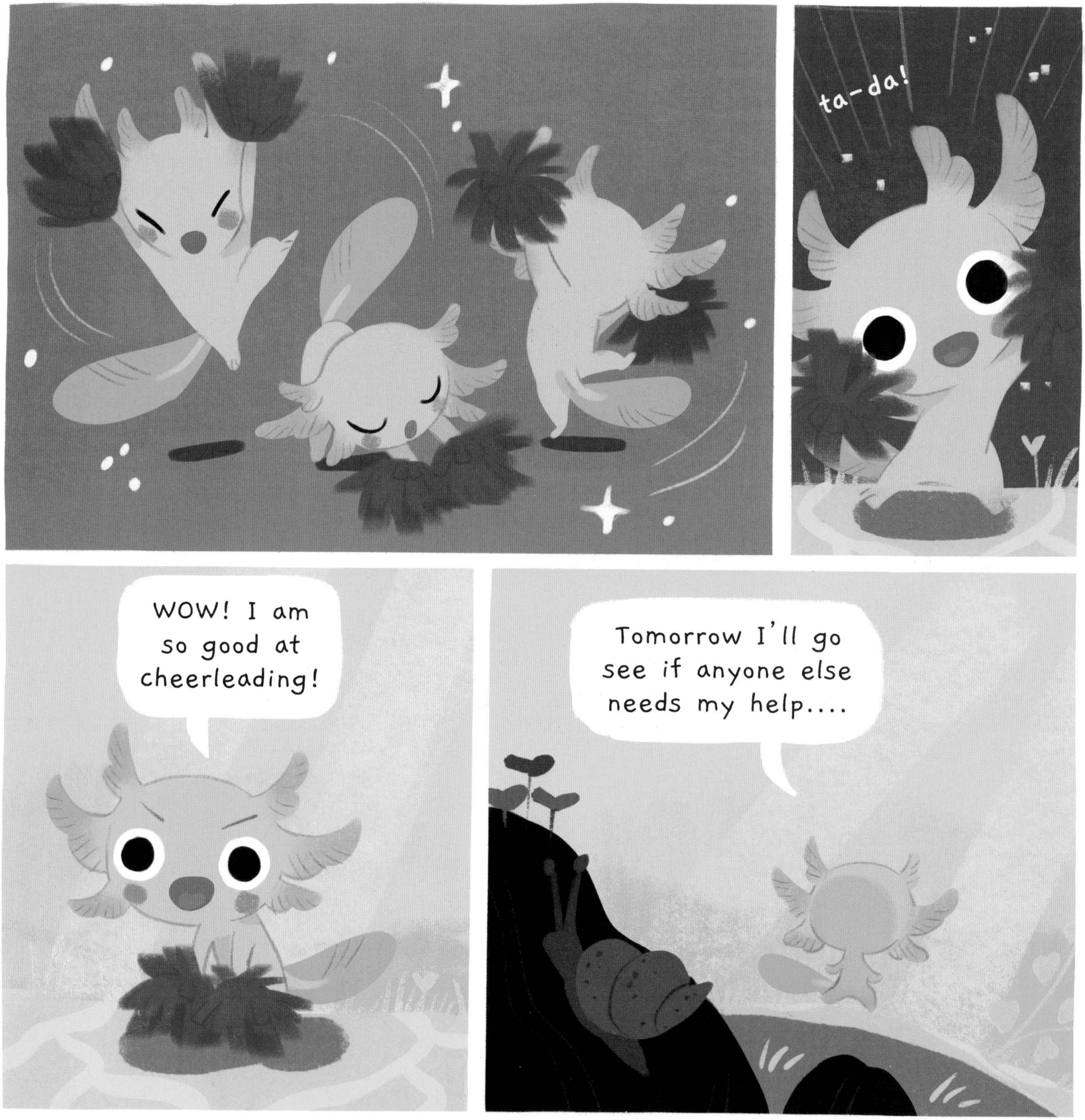
ta-da!
WOW! I am so good at cheerleading!
Tomorrow I'll go see if anyone else needs my help....

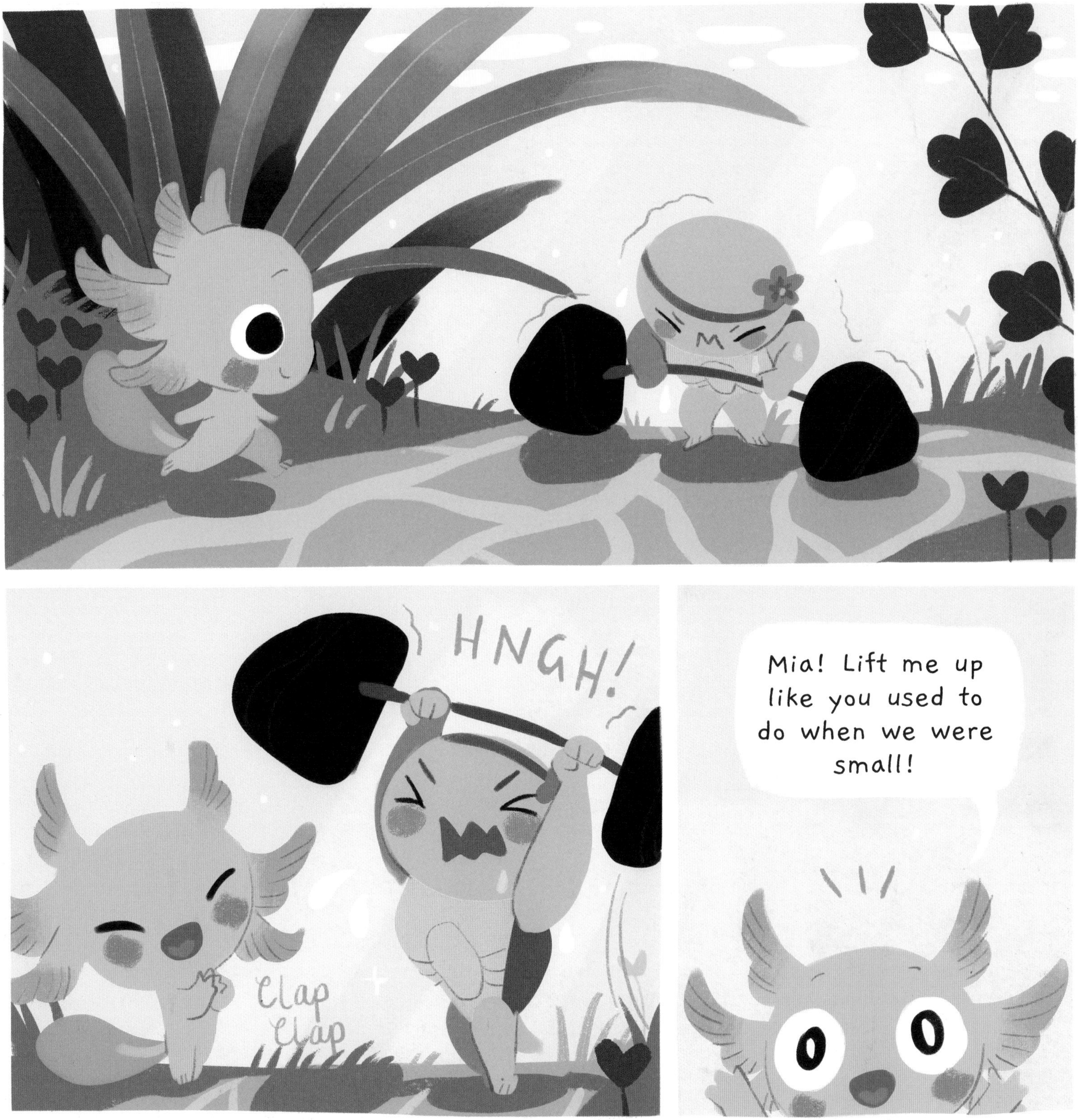
HNGH!
Clap
Clap
Mia! Lift me up like you used to do when we were small!

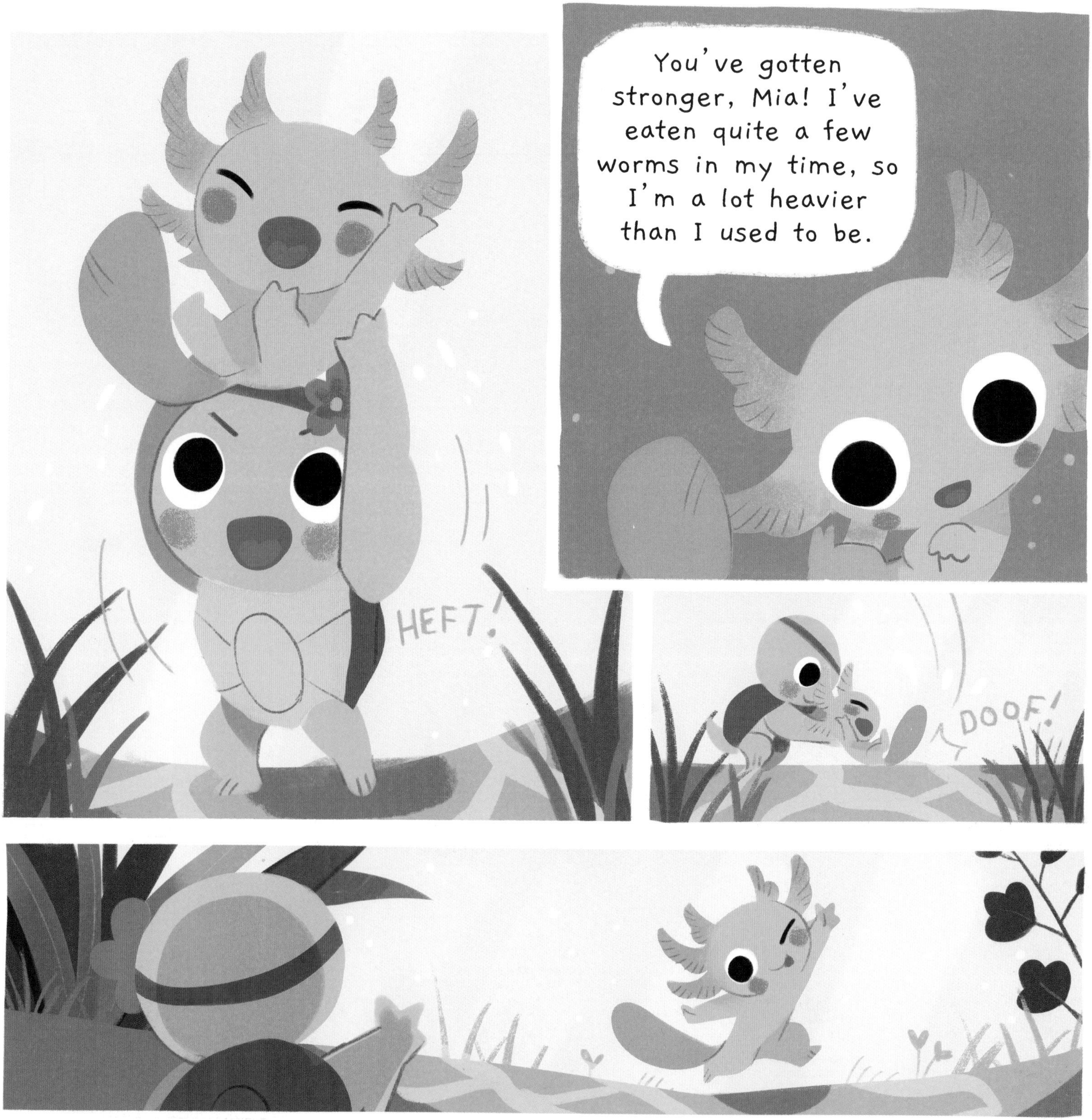
You've gotten stronger, Mia! I've eaten quite a few worms in my time, so I'm a lot heavier than I used to be.
HEFT!
DOOF!

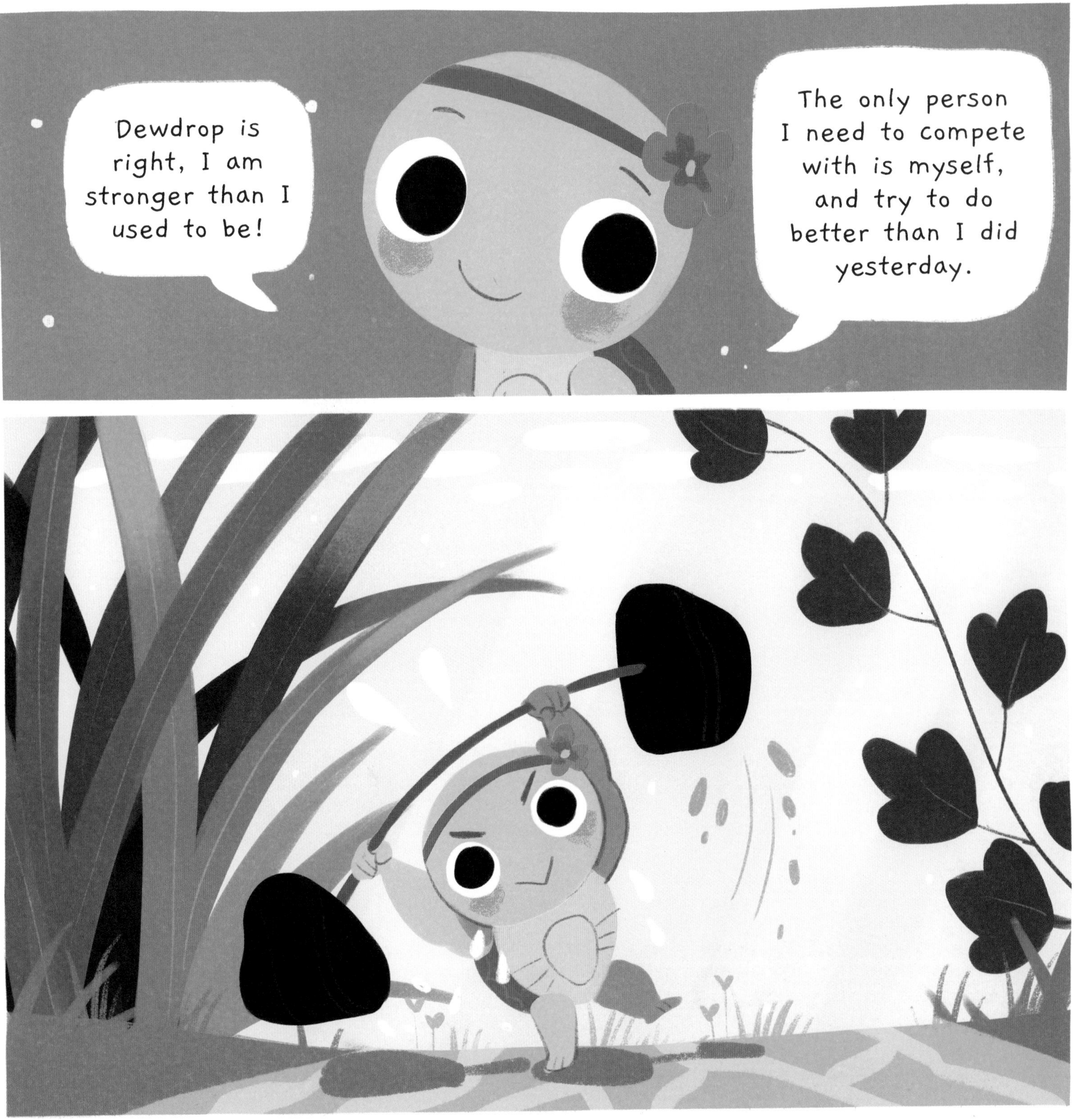
Dewdrop is right, I am stronger than I used to be!
The only person I need to compete with is myself, and try to do better than I did yesterday.

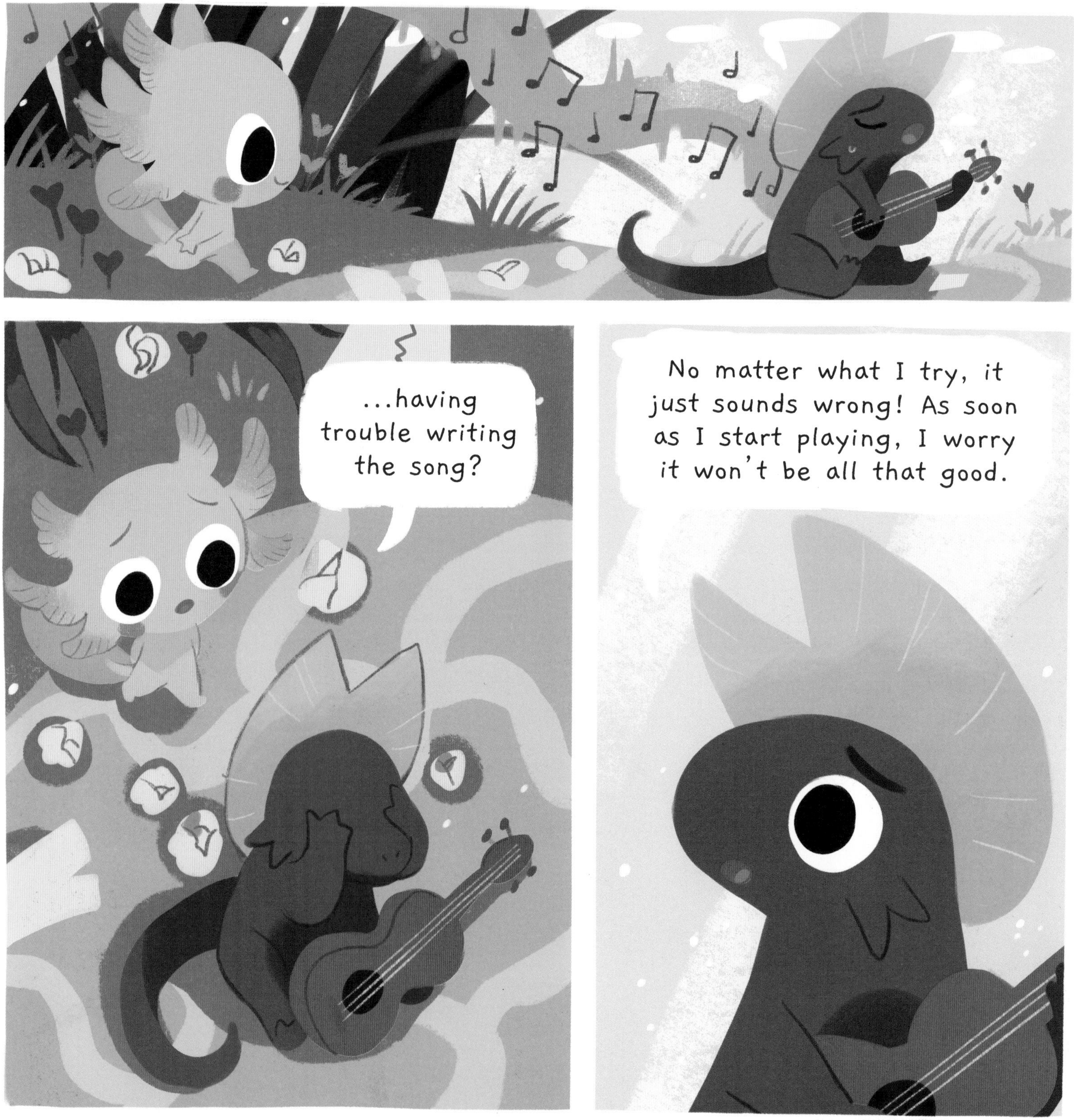
...having trouble writing the song?
No matter what I try, it just sounds wrong! As soon as I start playing, I worry it won't be all that good.

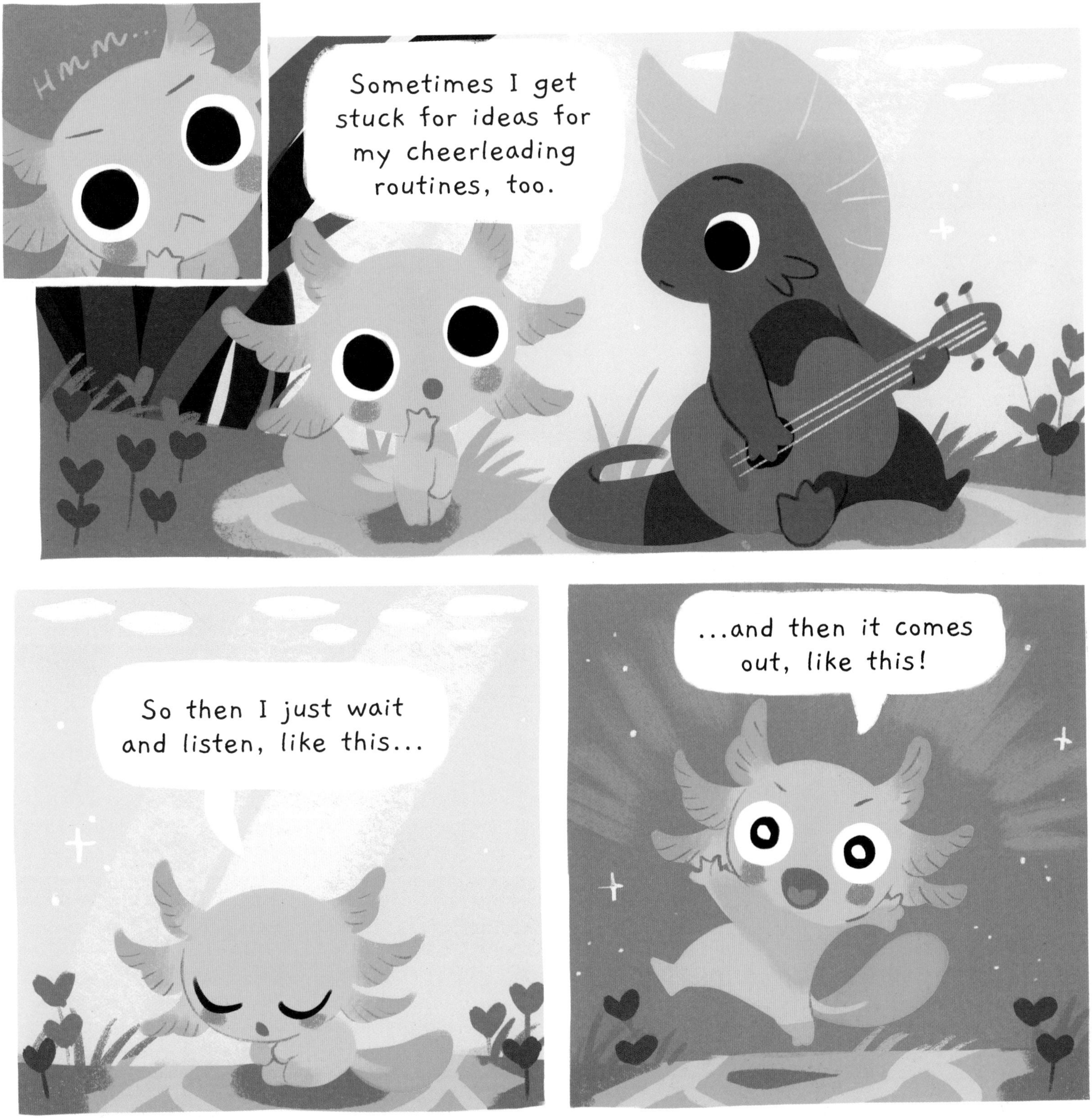
HMM...
Sometimes I get stuck for ideas for my cheerleading routines, too.
So then I just wait and listen, like this...
...and then it comes out, like this!

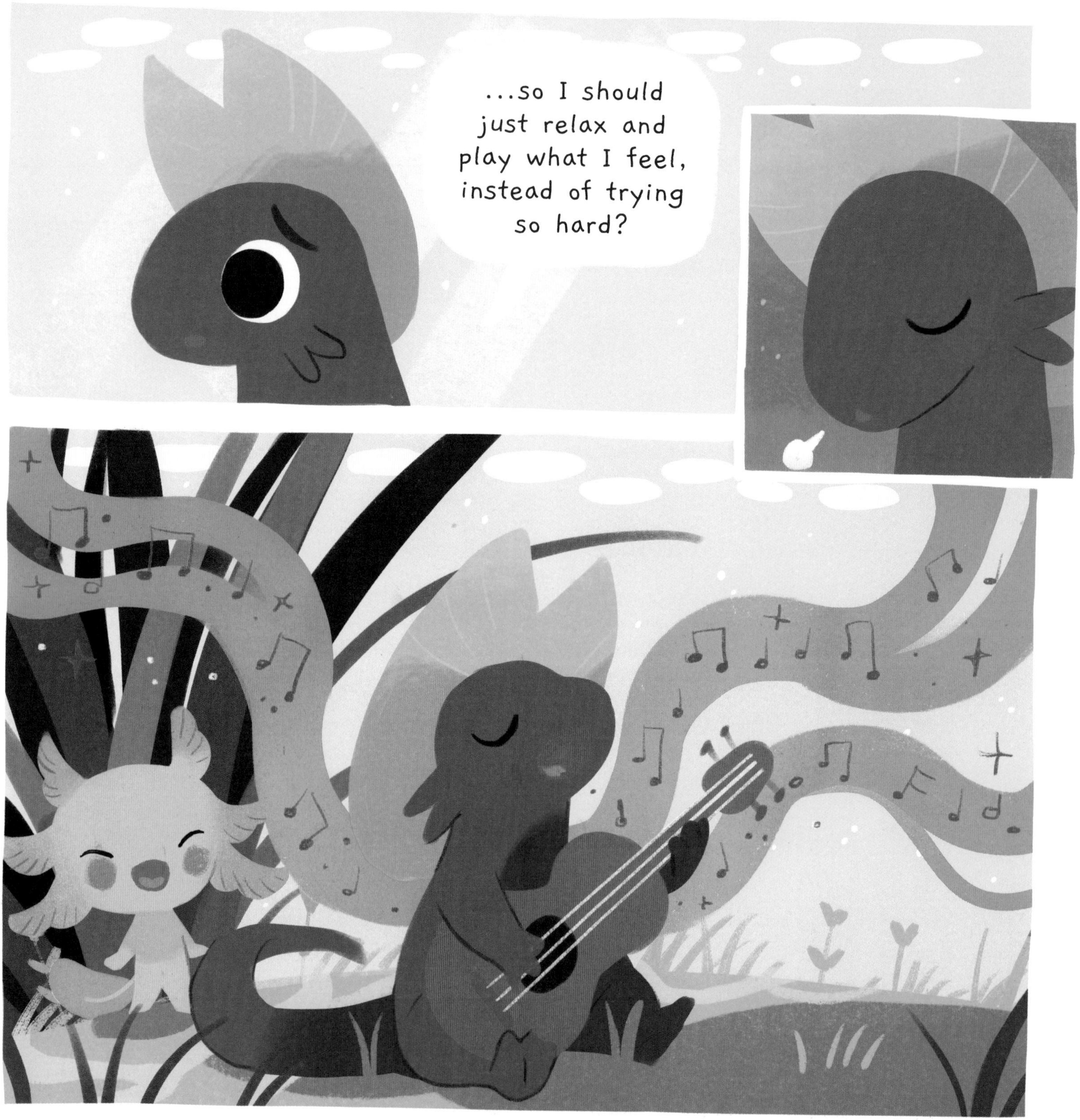
...so I should just relax and play what I feel, instead of trying so hard?

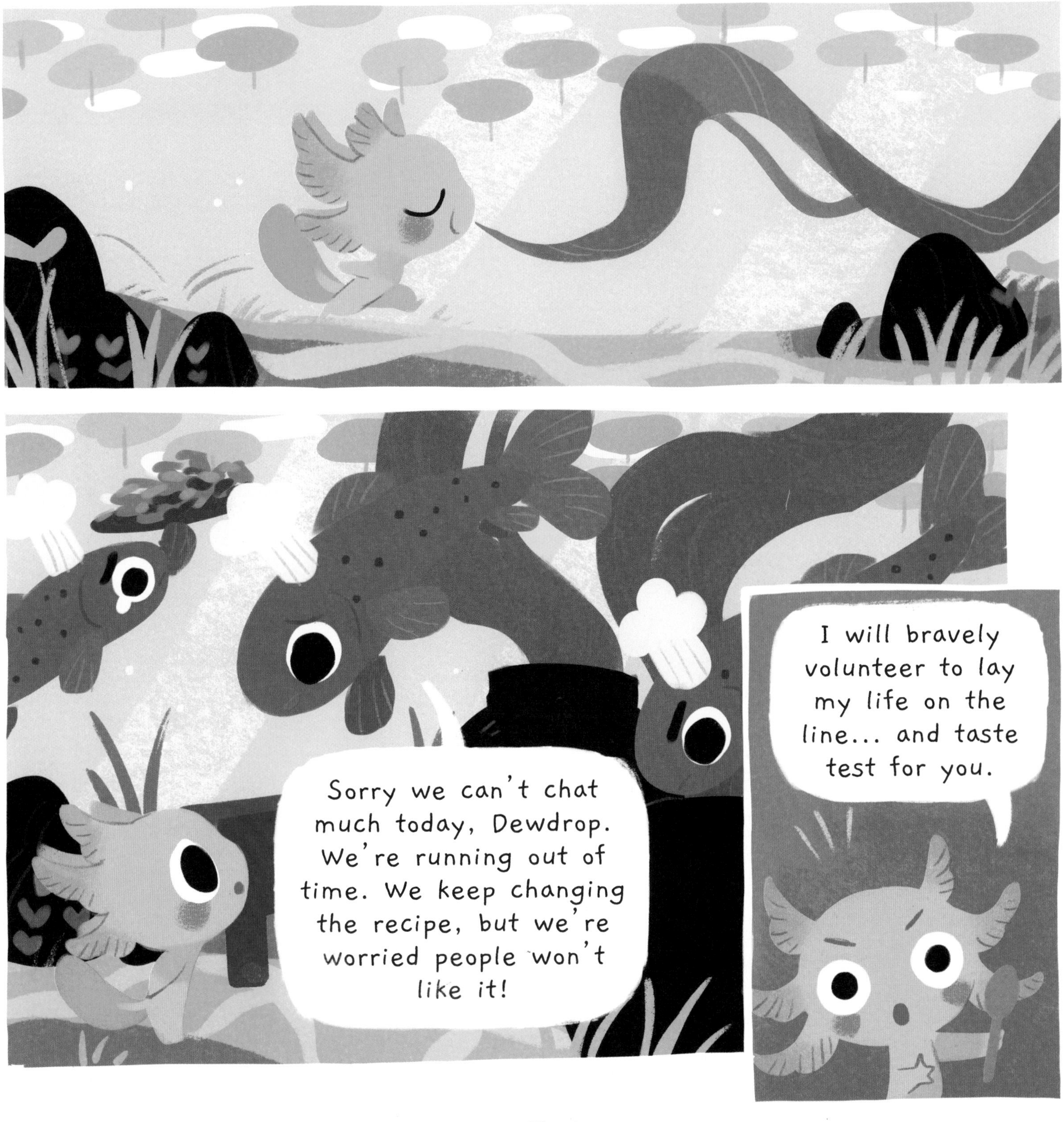
Sorry we can't chat much today, Dewdrop. We're running out of time. We keep changing the recipe, but we're worried people won't like it!
I will bravely volunteer to lay my life on the line... and taste test for you.

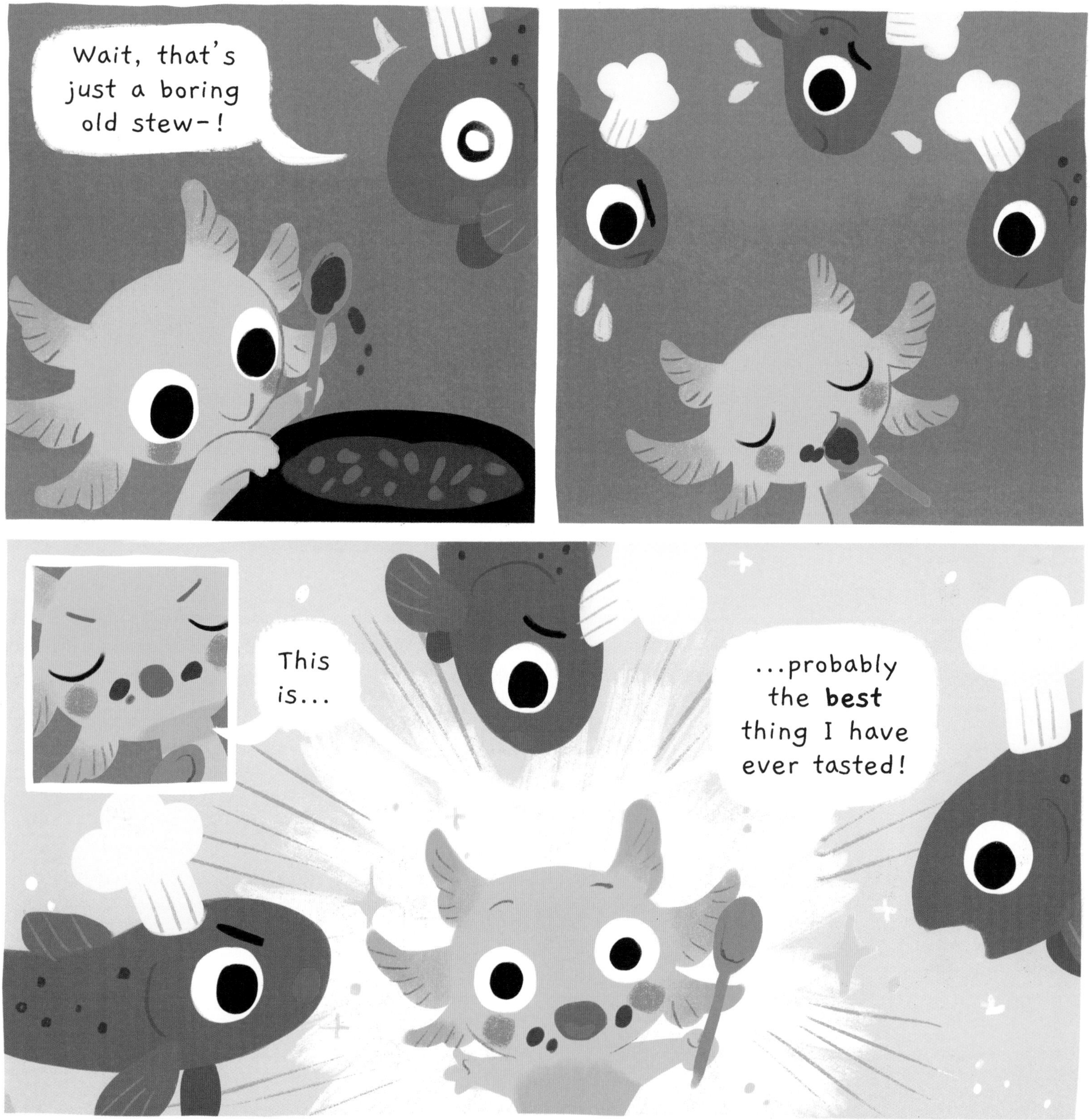
Wait, that's just a boring old stew-!
This is...
...probably the **best** thing I have ever tasted!

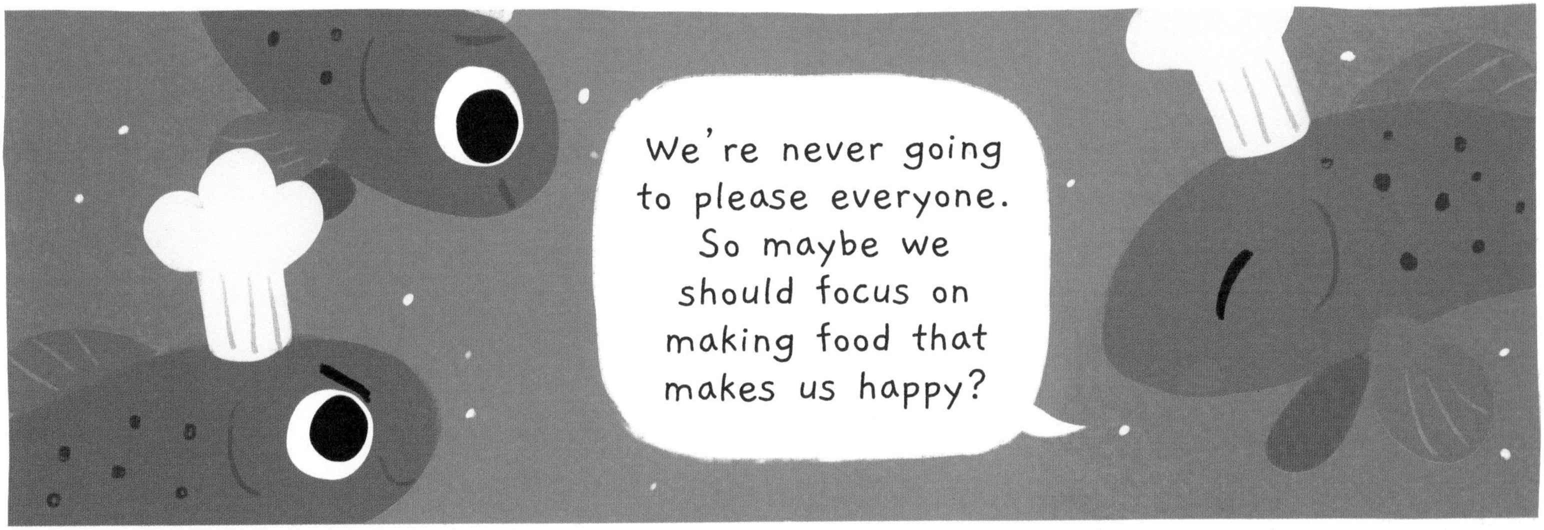
We're never going to please everyone. So maybe we should focus on making food that makes us happy?

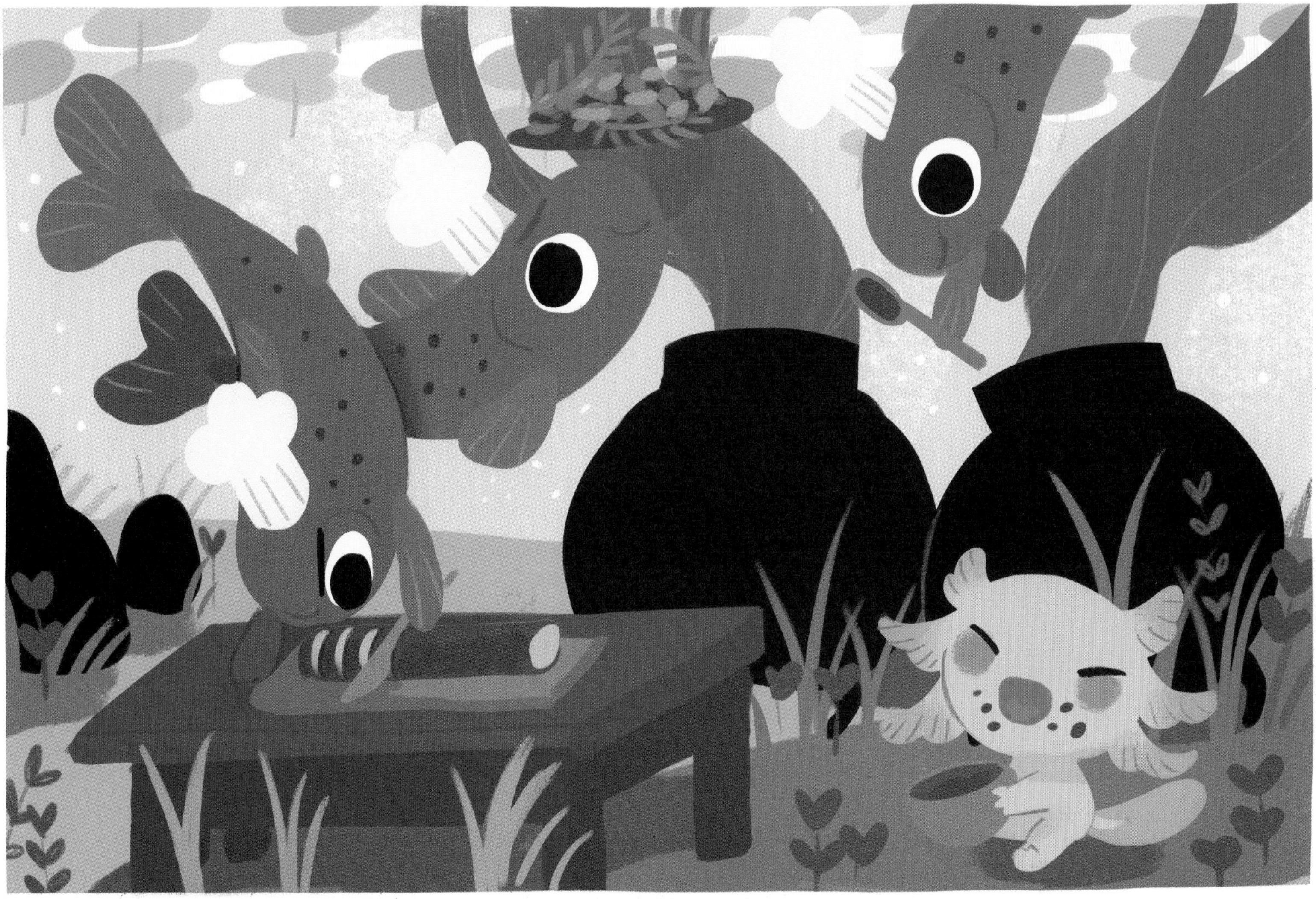

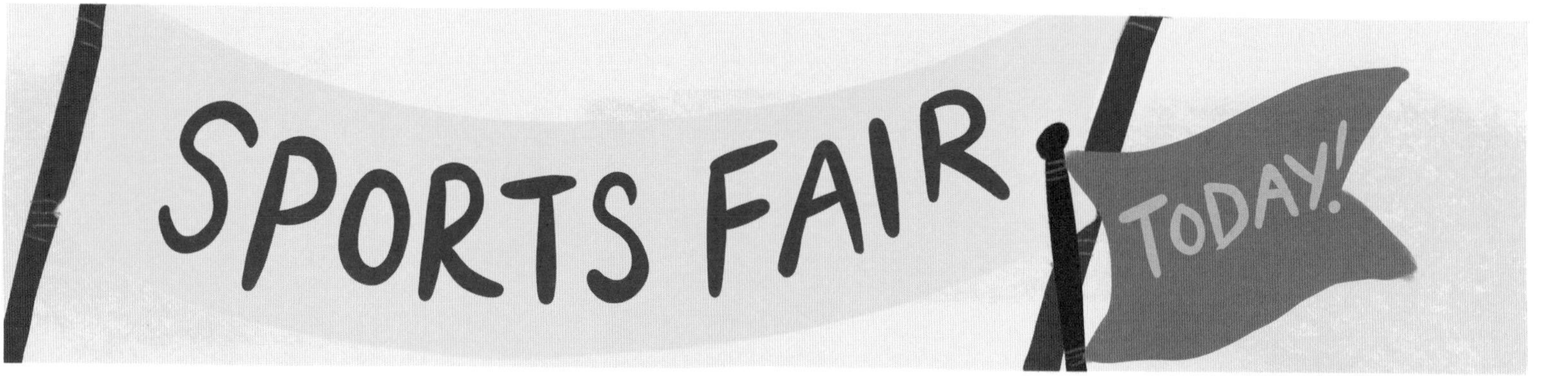
SPORTS FAIR
TODAY!

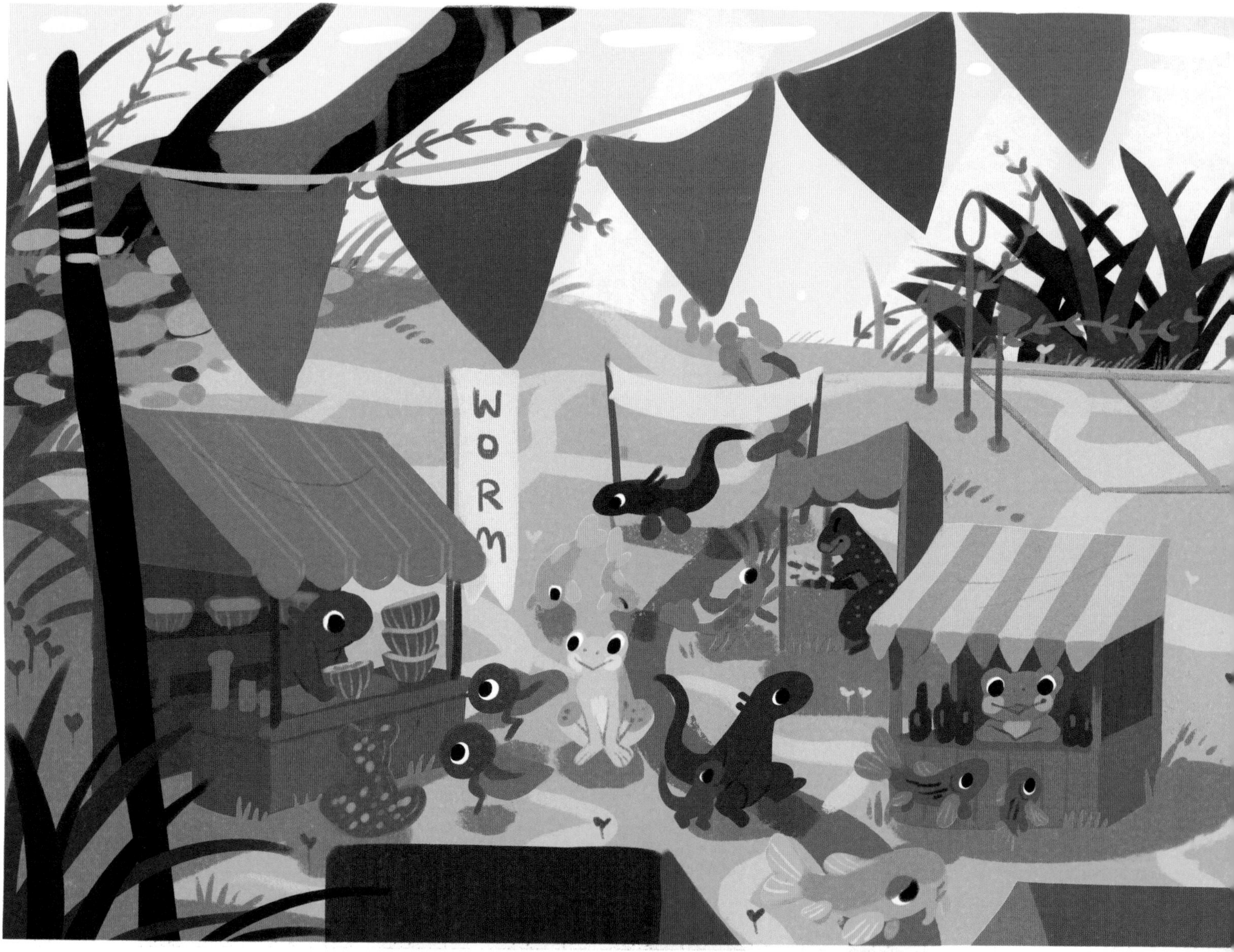
WORM

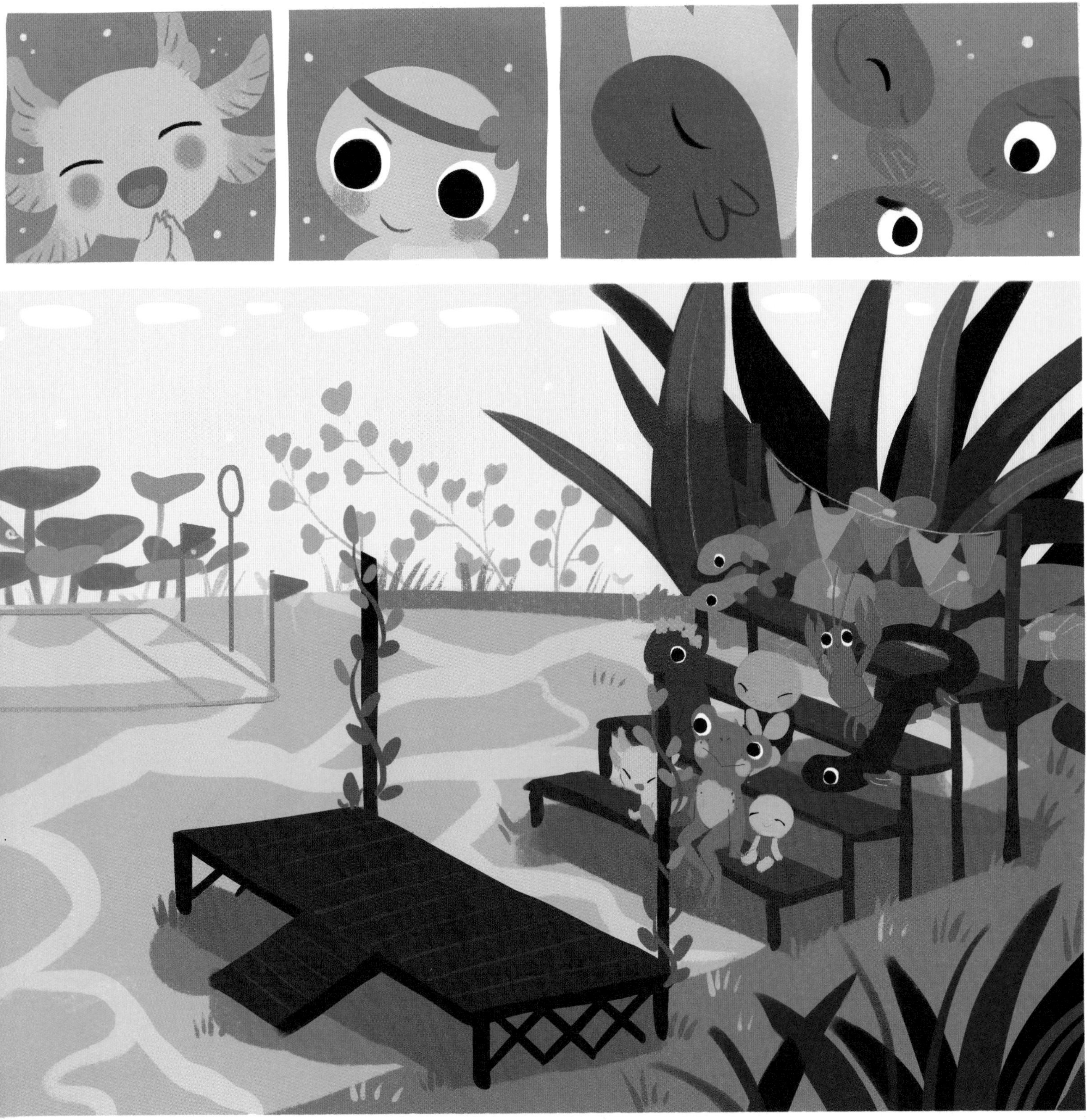

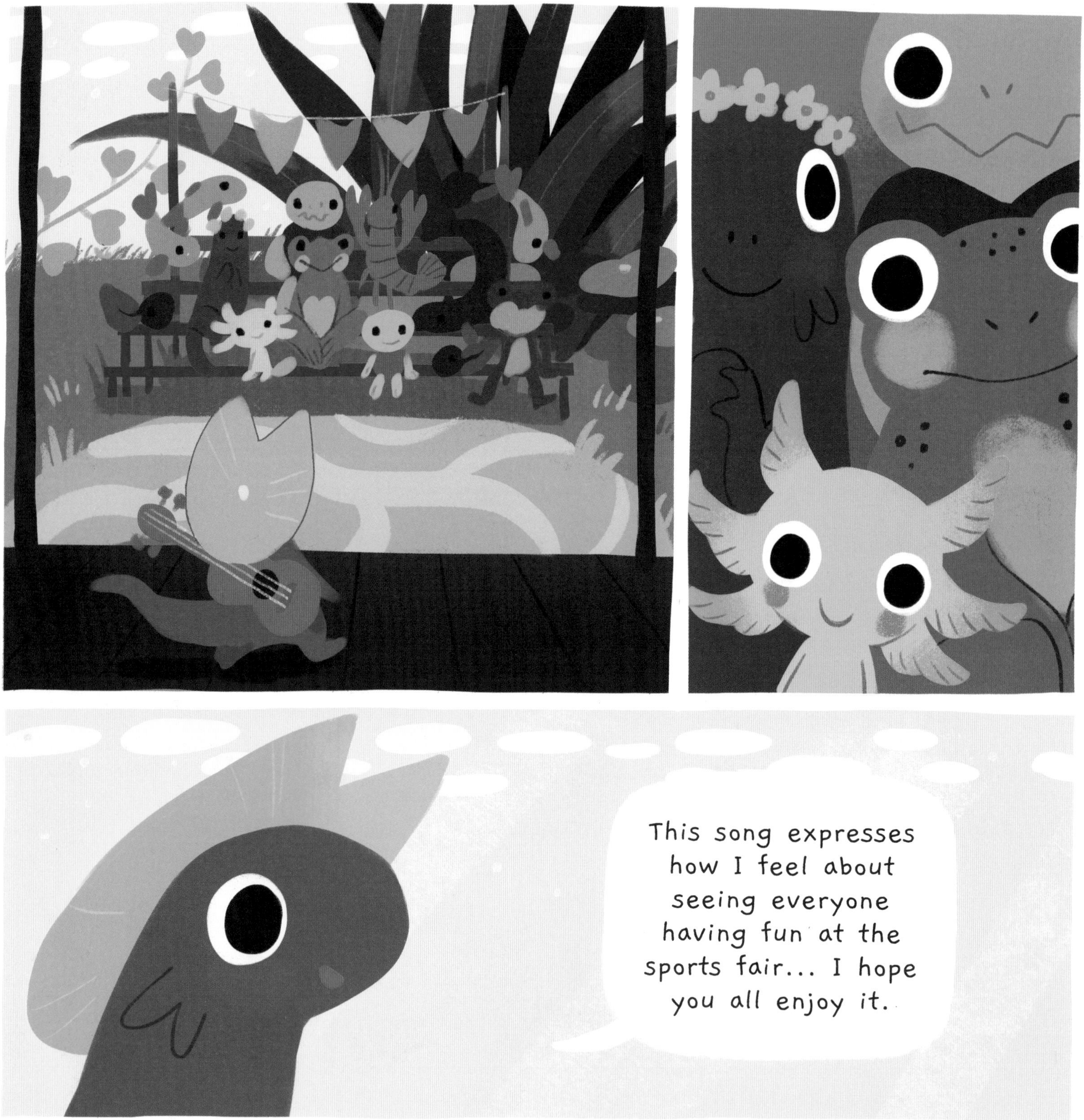
This song expresses how I feel about seeing everyone having fun at the sports fair... I hope you all enjoy it.

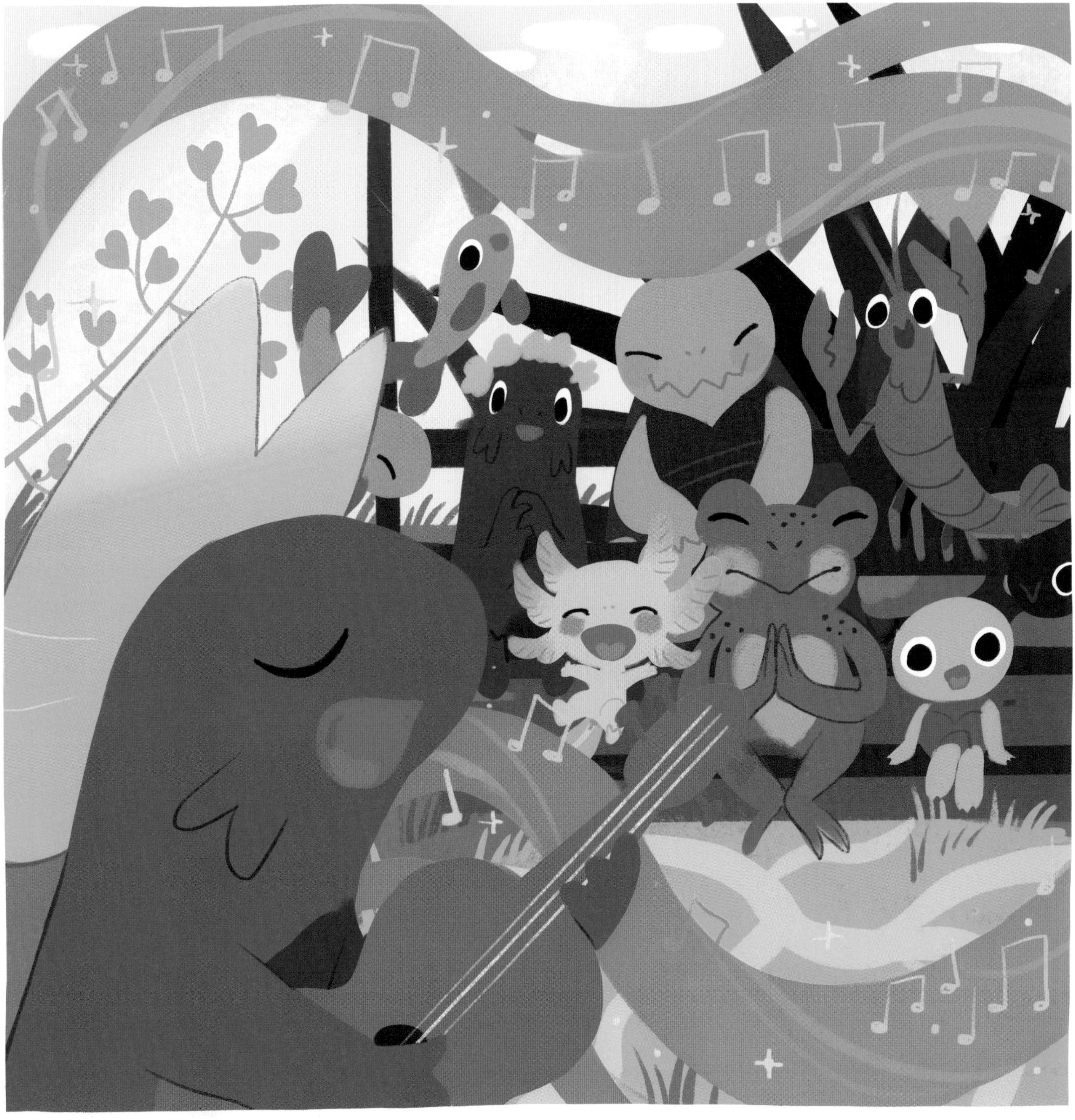

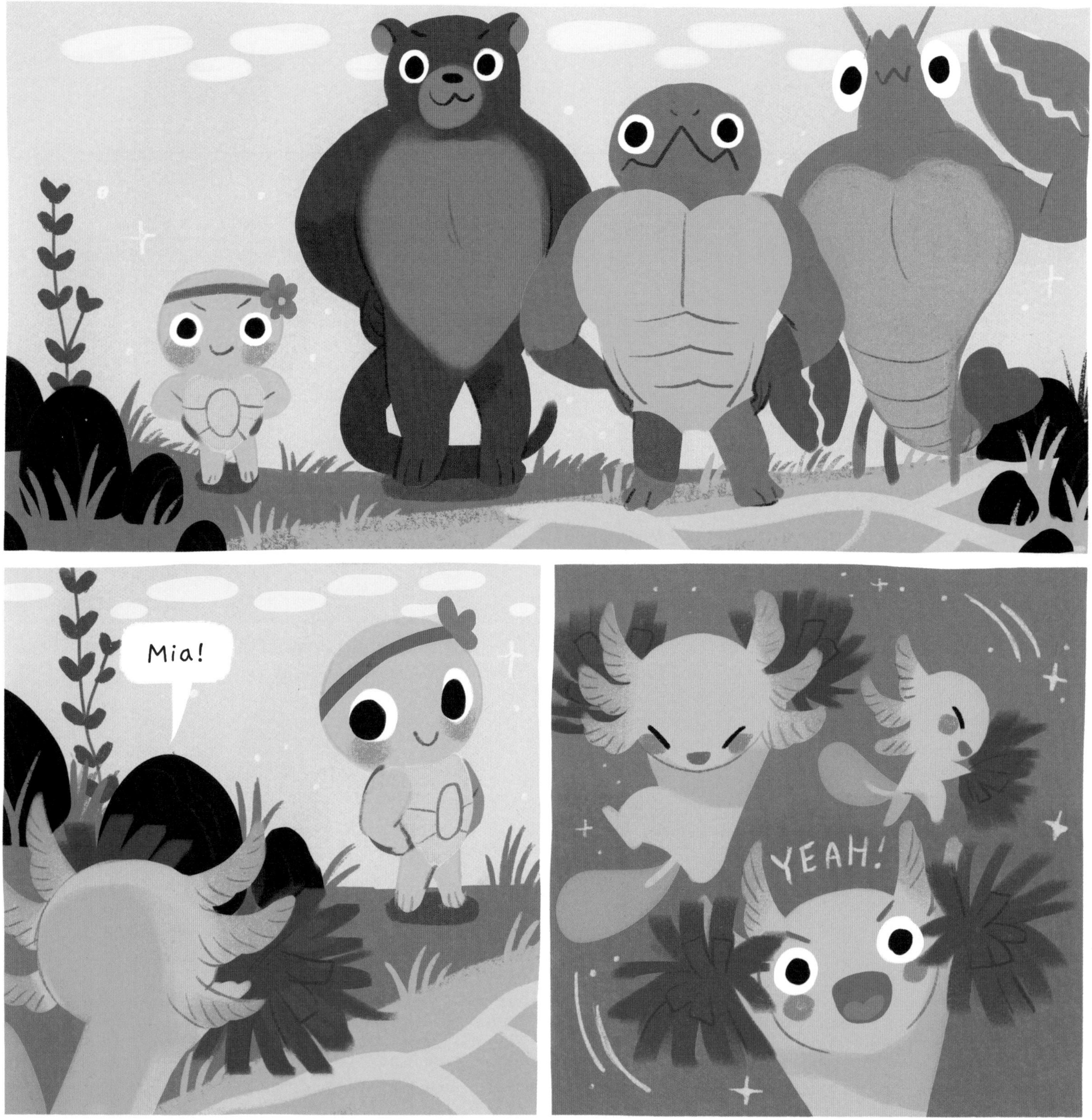
Mia!
YEAH!

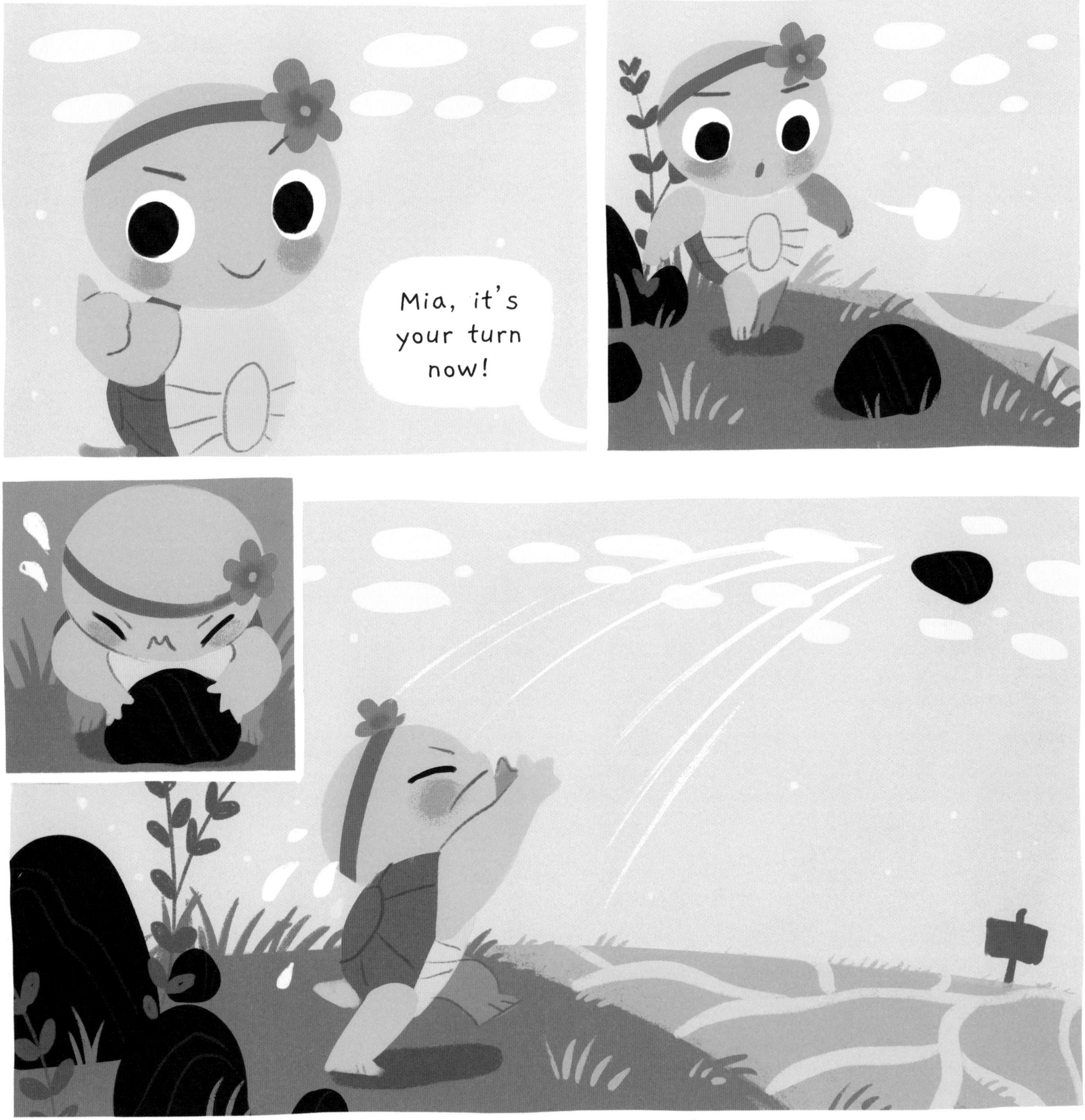
Mia, it's your turn now!

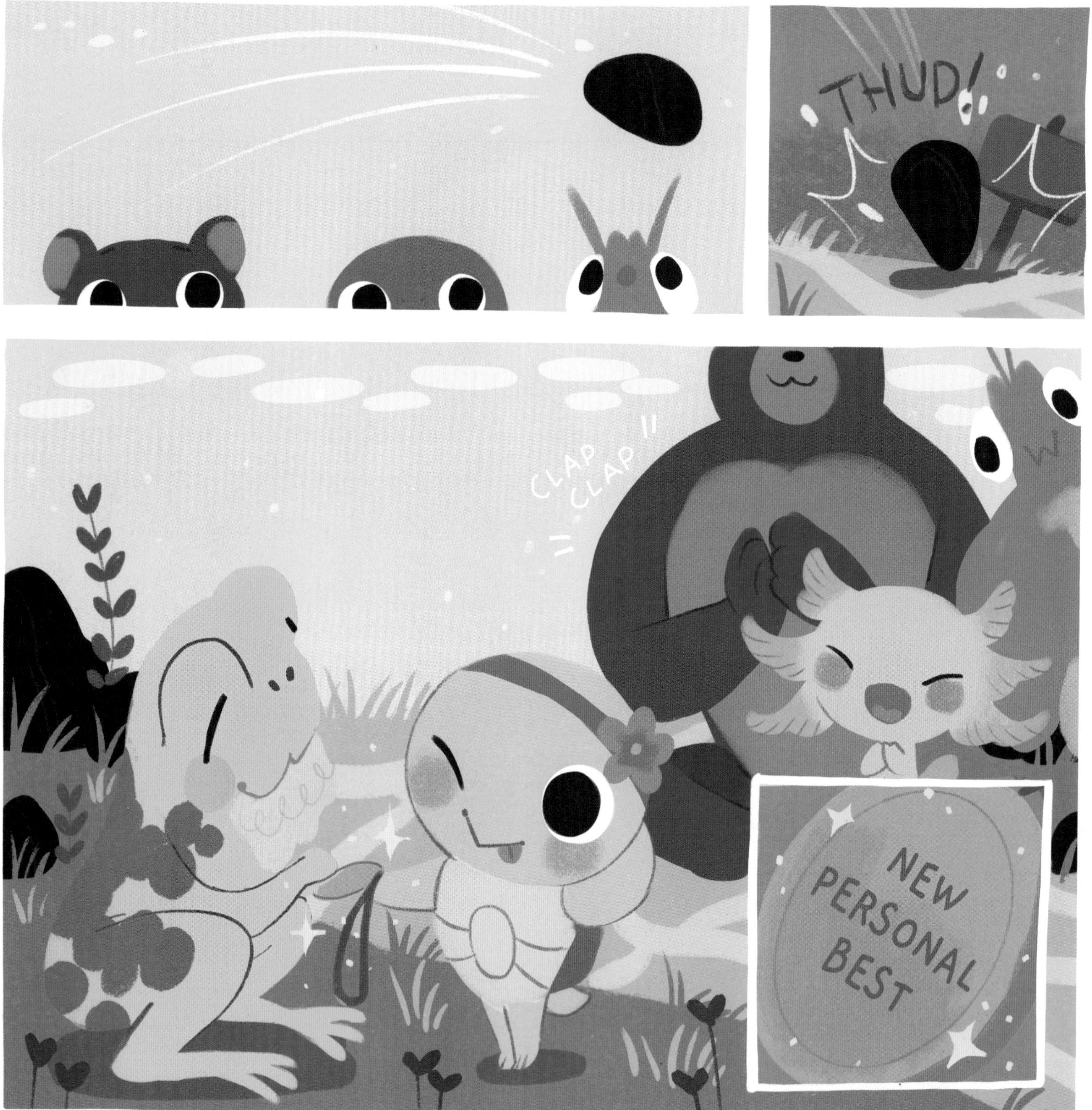
THUD!
CLAP CLAP
NEW PERSONAL BEST

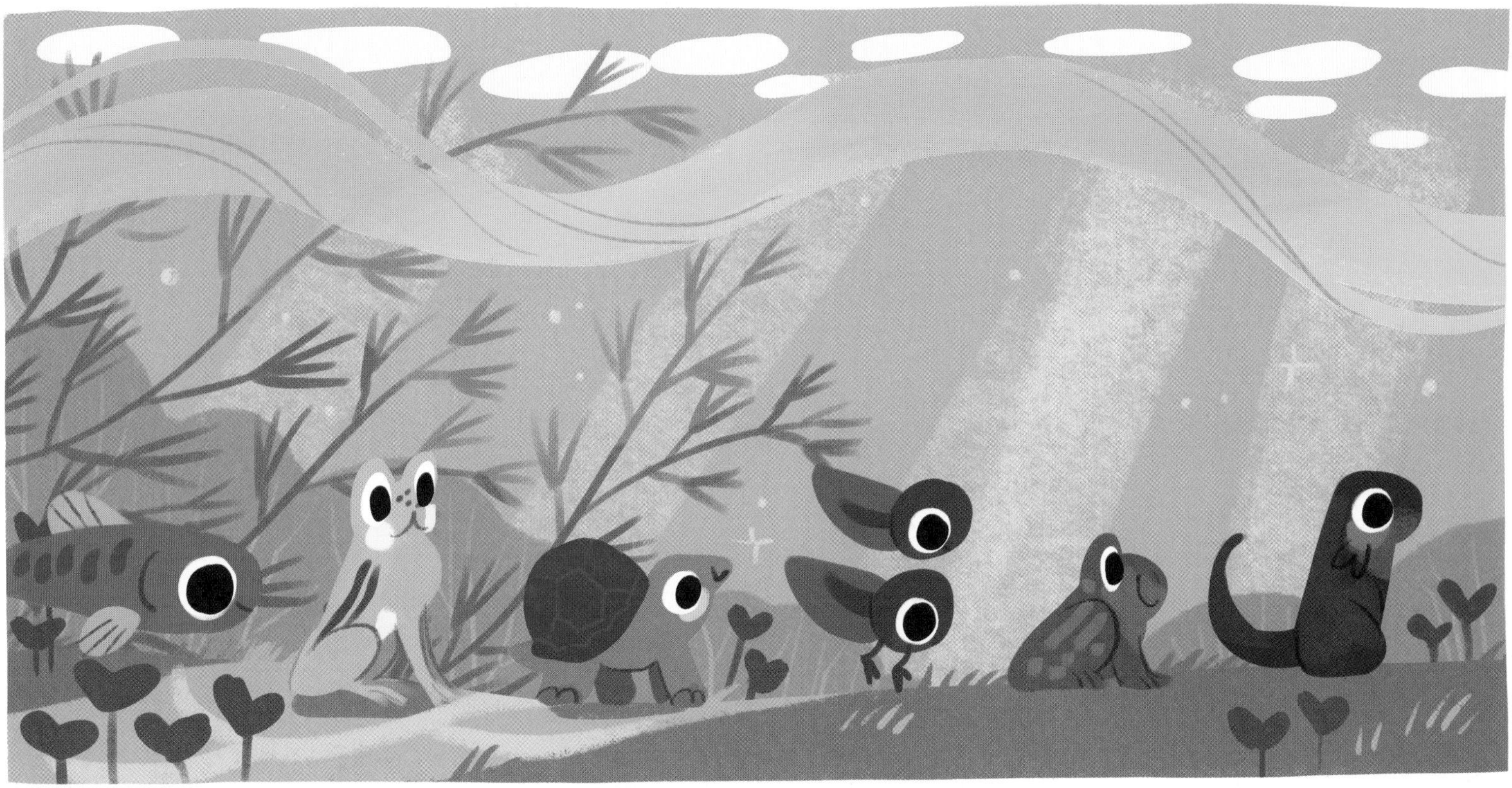

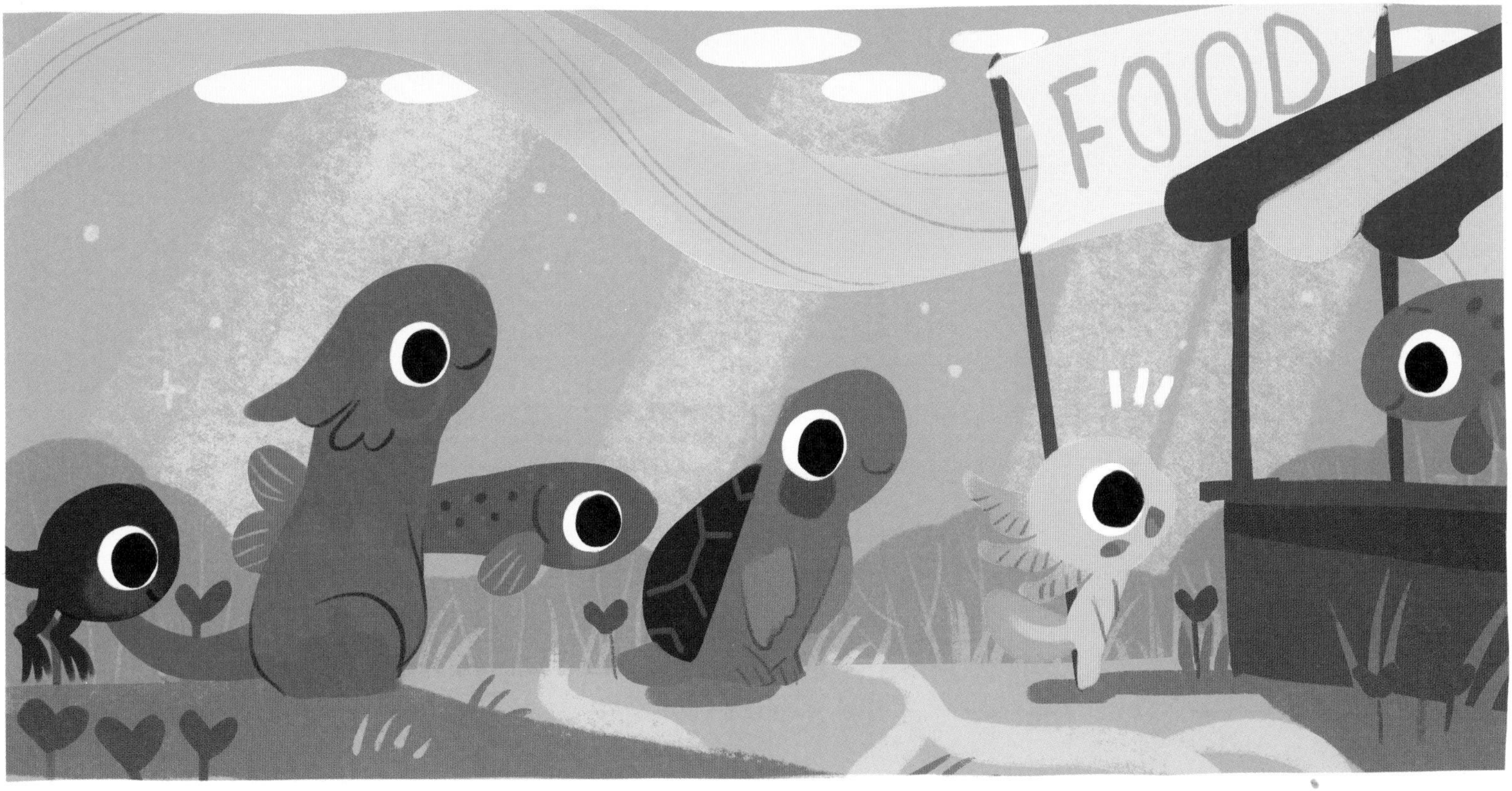
FOOD

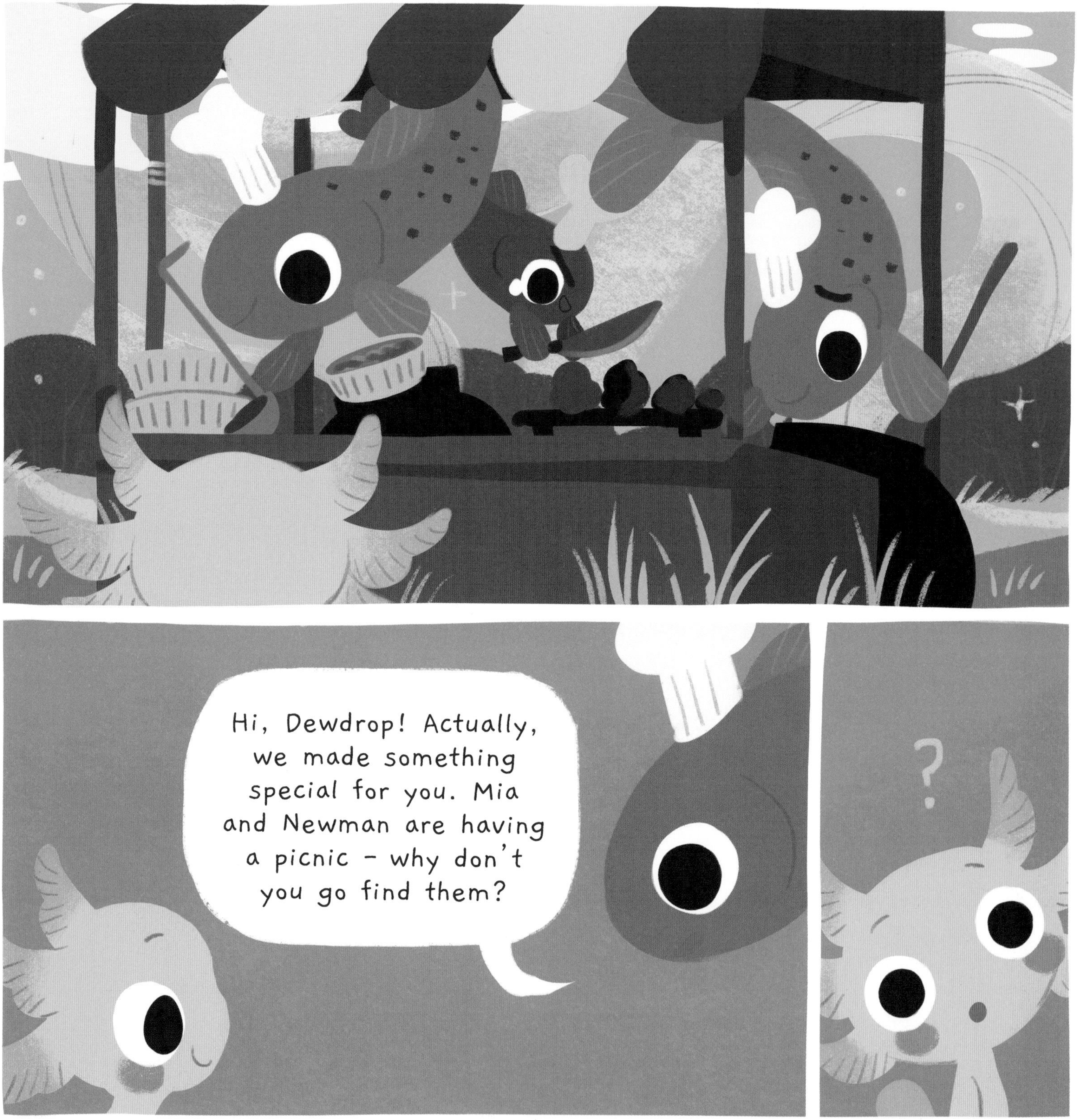
Hi, Dewdrop! Actually, we made something special for you. Mia and Newman are having a picnic - why don't you go find them?
?

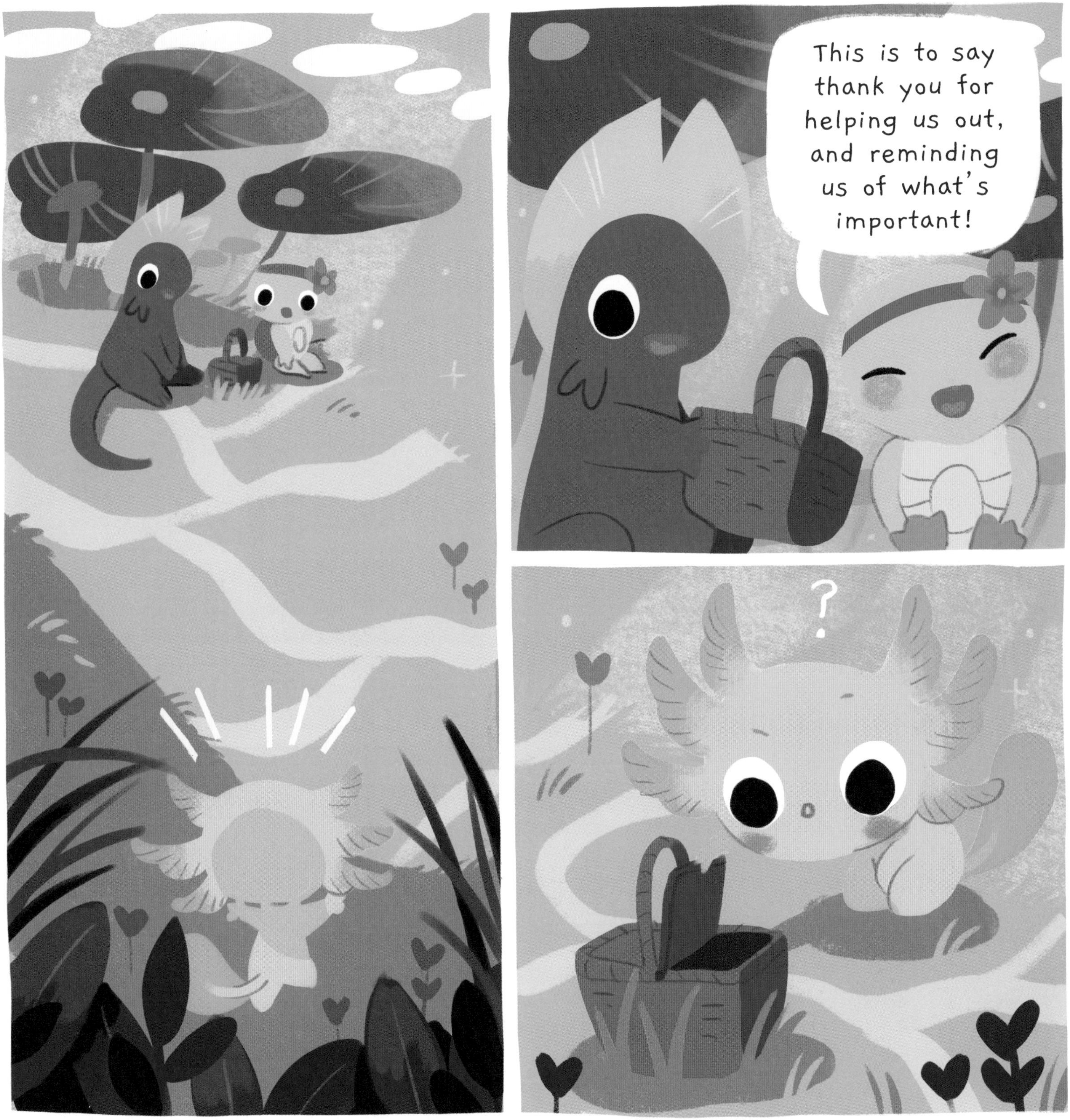
This is to say thank you for helping us out, and reminding us of what's important!
?

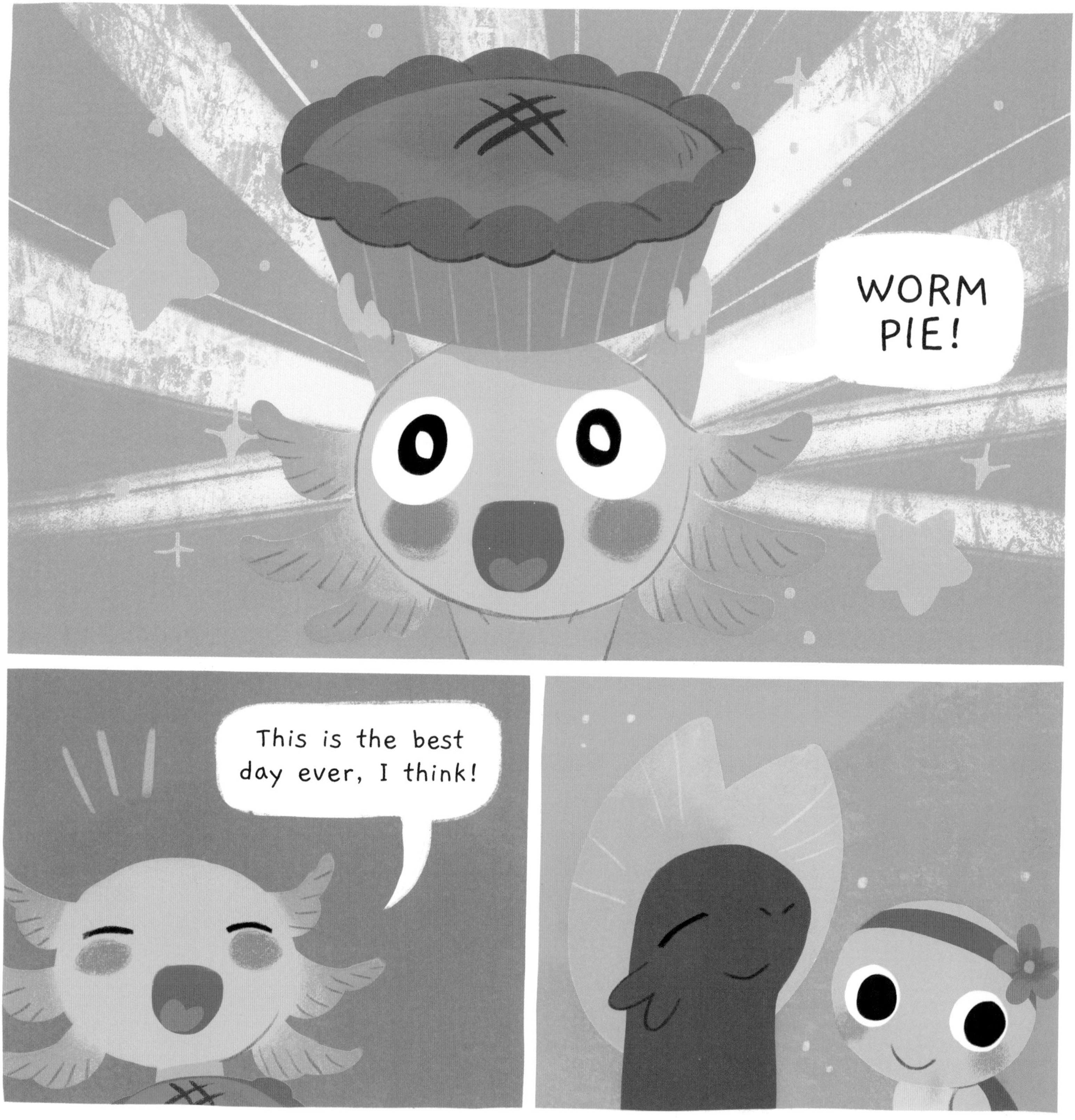
WORM PIE!
This is the best day ever, I think!

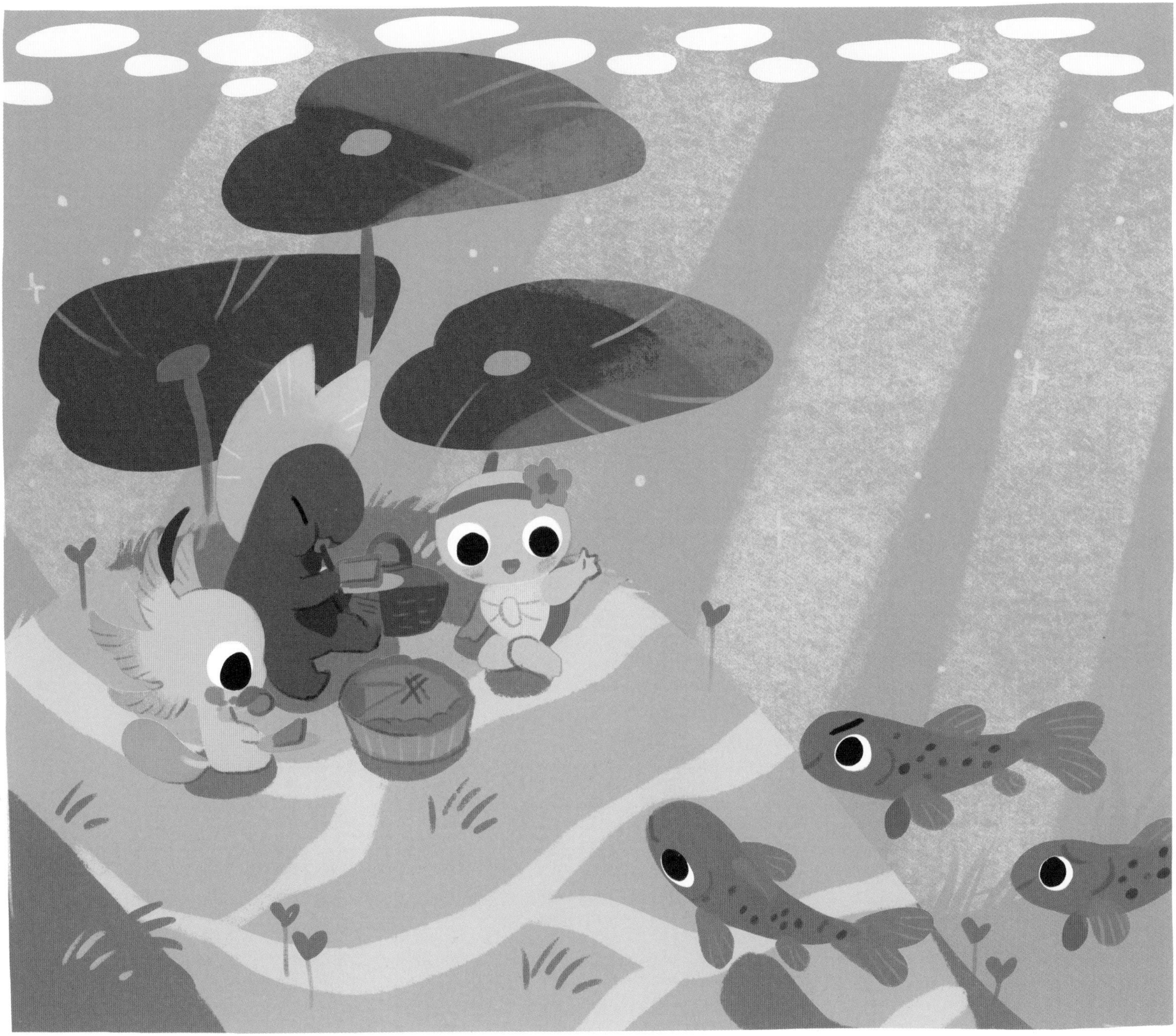

The End

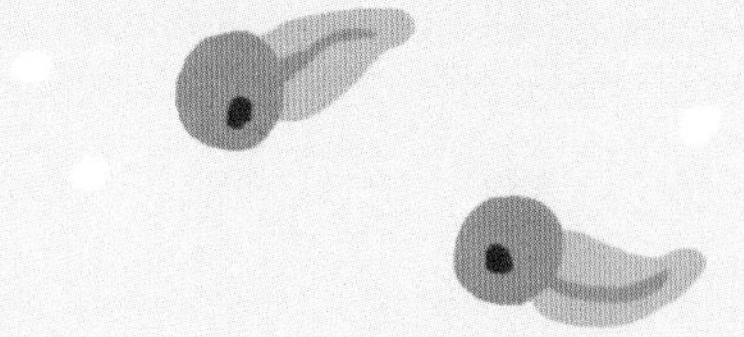

Want to know more about Dewdrop and his friends? Check out some fun animal facts in the next pages!

Ponds and rivers throughout the world provide wonderful homes for many different creatures. They have lots to eat, places to hide, and a safe space for raising young. However, all of this lives in a special balance. When humans add too much pollution, or drain ponds to build more housing, or introduce new species that aren't meant to live there, it can upset the balance. The result is that some pond and river-dwelling creatures are disappearing from the water and becoming endangered.

To help, you can learn about which species are native to waterways near you—meaning they are meant to live there. You can support local conservation projects by visiting them, donating, and telling people about how important they are. Sometimes they need volunteers to help replant or rebuild an area, so you can help that way too.

It's important for us to use our voices to protect the lives and homes of creatures who don't have a voice themselves.

Dewdrop is an axolotl!

Facts about axolotls:

- They live in the water for their whole life
- They have no teeth
- They can regrow parts of their bodies if they get hurt
- They love to eat worms, and anything else that can fit in their mouth

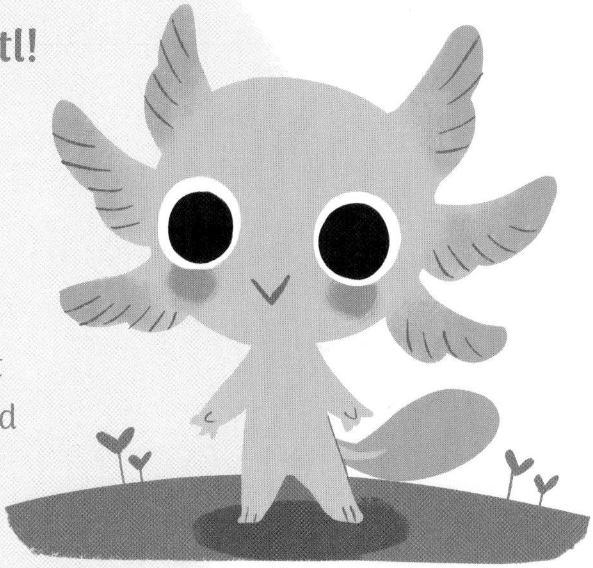

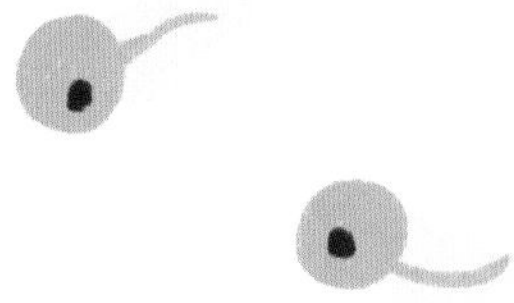

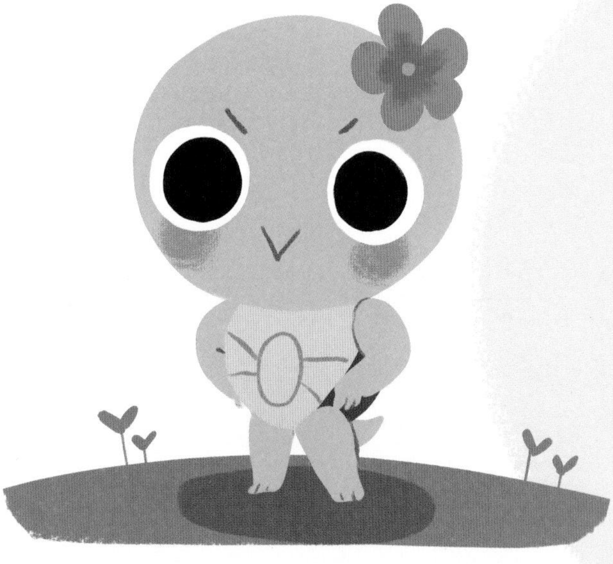

Mia is a yellow-bellied slider, which is a type of turtle!

Facts about turtles:

- They lay eggs
- They have hard shells to protect them, and most turtles can hide inside their shell if there's danger
- They like to dry out their shell with a nice afternoon of sunbathing
- The largest turtle is the leatherback sea turtle, which can weigh over 2,000 pounds

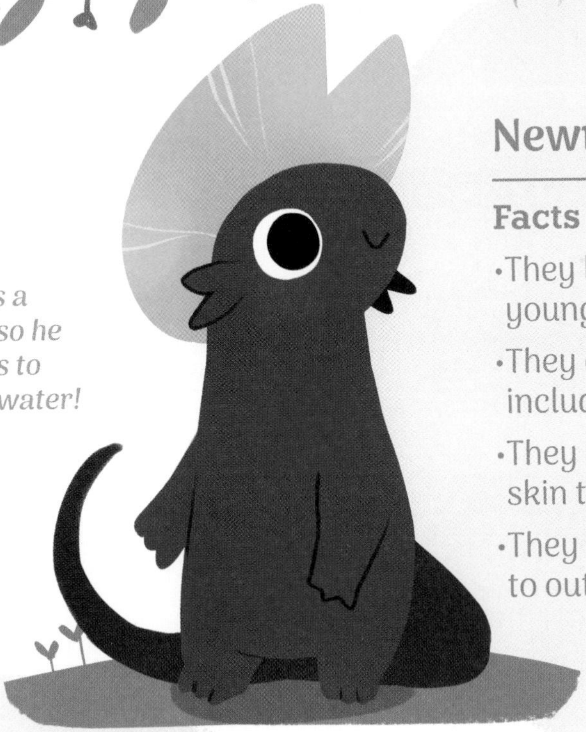

Newman is a young newt, so he still has gills to breathe underwater!

Newman is a newt!

Facts about newts:

- They live in the water when they are young, and on land when they are older
- They can be lots of different colors, including bright colors like orange or red
- They can sometimes make a poison in their skin to protect them from being eaten
- They have flown on missions to outer space

The cooks are minnows!

Facts about minnows:

- They are the largest freshwater fish family in the world, with thousands of different species
- They are usually very small
- They are often used for bait in fishing
- They can be very picky eaters, using taste and touch to figure out whether they want to eat something

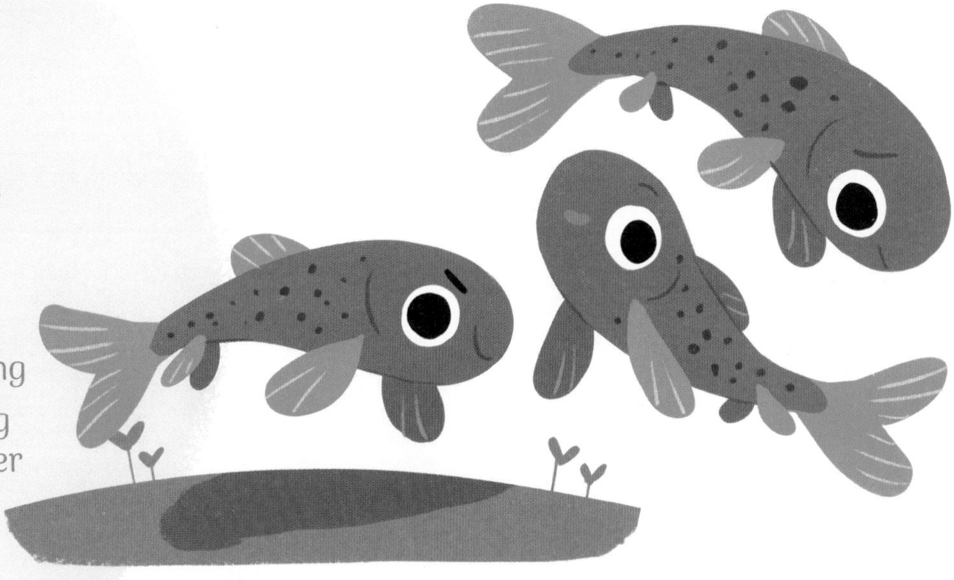

Also from Katie O'Neill

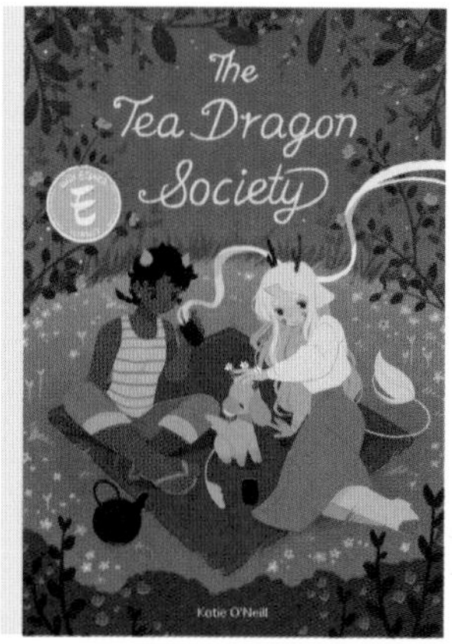
The Tea Dragon Society
Katie O'Neill

THE TEA DRAGON SOCIETY

The Eisner Award-winning gentle fantasy that follows the story of Greta, a blacksmith apprentice, and the people she meets as she becomes entwined in the enchanting world of Tea Dragons.

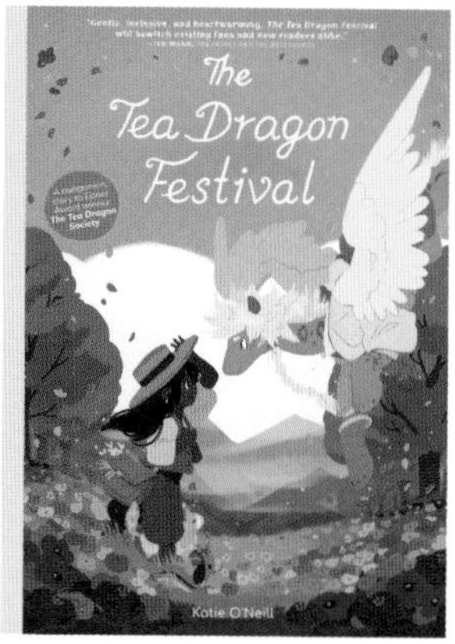
The Tea Dragon Festival
Katie O'Neill

THE TEA DRAGON FESTIVAL

Rinn has grown up with the Tea Dragons that inhabit their village, but stumbling across a real dragon turns out to be a different matter entirely! A charming story about finding your purpose, and the community that helps you along the way.

THE TEA DRAGON SOCIETY CARD GAME

Create a bond between yourself and your Tea Dragon in this easy-to-learn card game based on the graphic novel!

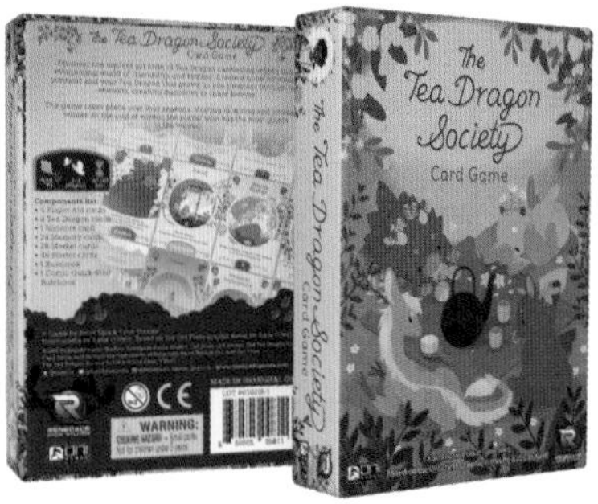
The Tea Dragon Society
Card Game

AQUICORN COVE BOARD GAME

Work with your friends to keep the reef healthy while taking care of your village in this cooperative board game based on the graphic novel!

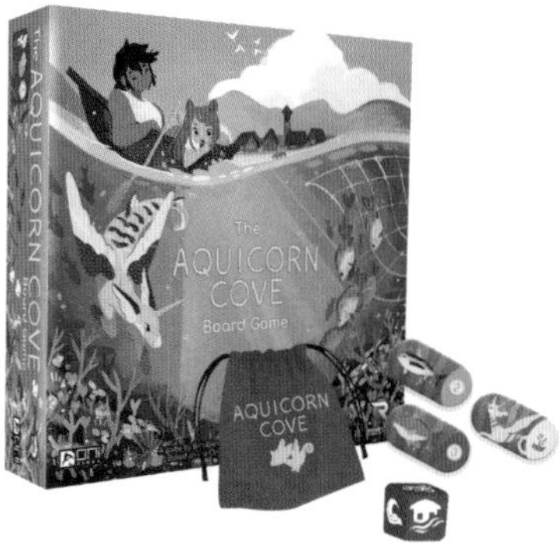
The Aquicorn Cove
Board Game
AQUICORN COVE

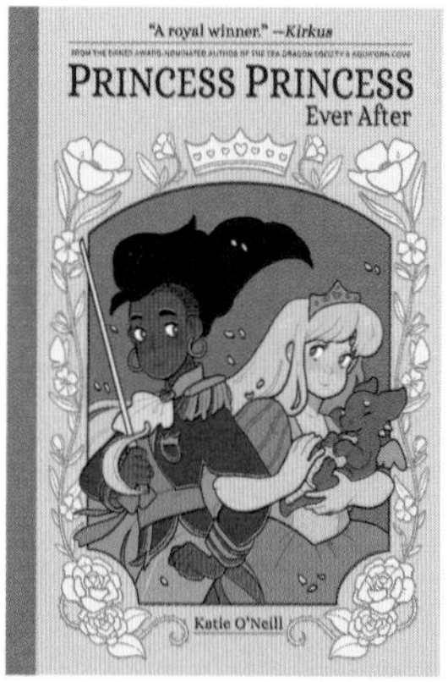
"A royal winner." —Kirkus
PRINCESS PRINCESS
Ever After
Katie O'Neill

PRINCESS PRINCESS EVER AFTER

Join Sadie and Amira, two very different princesses with very different strengths, on their journey to figure out what "happily ever after" really means—and how they can find it with each other.

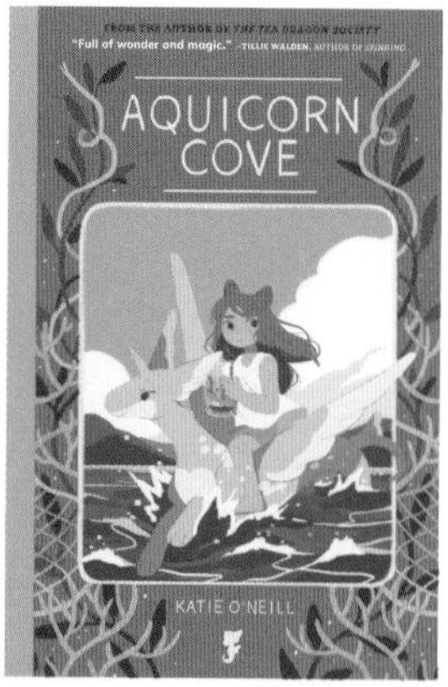
"Full of wonder and magic."
AQUICORN COVE
KATIE O'NEILL

AQUICORN COVE

Unable to rely on the adults in her storm-ravaged seaside town, a young girl named Lana must protect a colony of magical seahorse-like creatures she discovers in the coral reef.

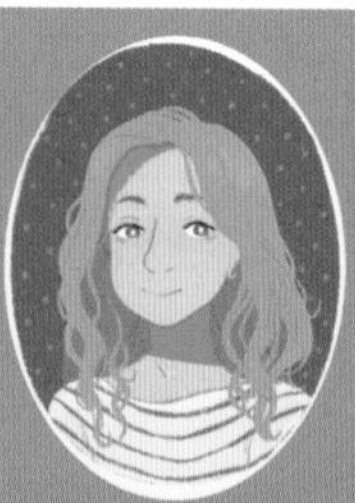

Katie O'Neill is an illustrator and graphic novelist from New Zealand, and author of *Princess Princess Ever After, Aquicorn Cove, The Tea Dragon Society, The Tea Dragon Festival,* and *Dewdrop*, all from Oni Press. She makes gentle fantasy stories for younger readers, and is very interested in tea, creatures, things that grow, and the magic of everyday life.

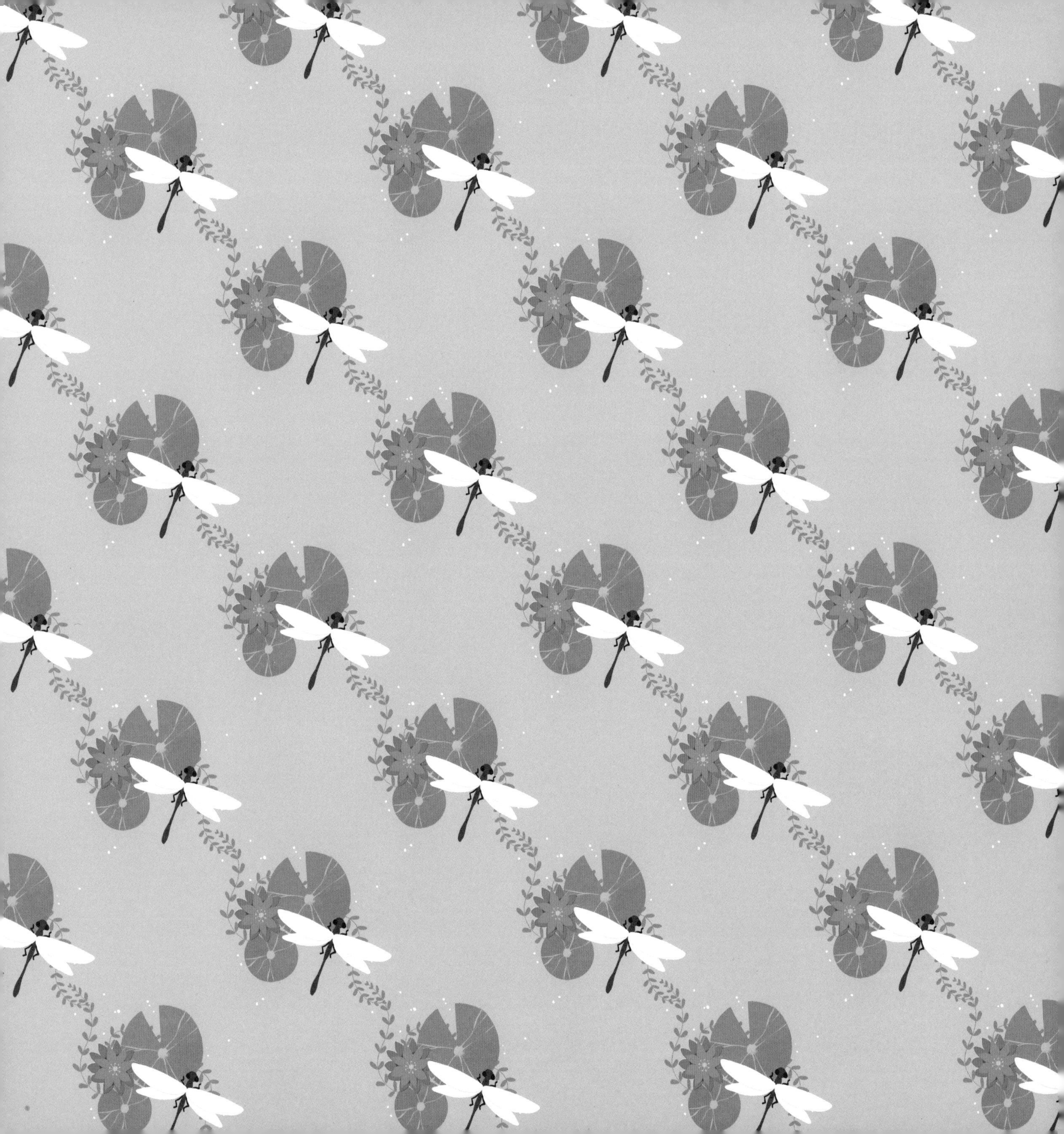